GiRL FROM THE QUEENDOM

Duck:
603-496-8948

GIRL FROM THE QUEENDOM: A Chapter Book

By Anna Watson | Laz-E-Femme Press

Design by Michael Mahin
Illustrations by Skye Murie

Published by Laz-E-Femme Press, Arlington, MA

www.lazefemmepress.weebly.com

ISBN (e-book): 978-0-9960304-3-4
ISBN (trade paperback): 978-09960304-2-7

Laz-E-Femme *Press*
All genres. All ages.
Queer voices.
Our stories.
Kick off your pumps and read!

For Devon

TABLE OF CONTENTS

GiRL FROM THE QUEENDOM

ANNA WATSON

CHAPTER ONE:
THE DEAL

The Endo-Patterson family was leaving Vermont. They were moving out of their big old farmhouse, Holy Smoke, where Jess and her brothers had been born. All weekend, friends and neighbors had been helping the E-P's load a moving van with a million boxes and bags, and now the rooms in Holy Smoke were just about empty. They made sad echoes when you walked. Cam and Hank, who were four, spent a lot of time marching around chanting, "AAHLINTON MASSACHOOSETS," which was where the E-Ps were moving. Moving away from the best place in the world—all because of the stupid Deal.

The deal with the Deal was this: when Jess's moms, Mugsy and Ka-chan, fell in love and wanted to get married and have kids, Ka-chan agreed to start out at Holy Smoke. This was because Mugsy was a true-blue Vermonter and Holy Smoke was her ancestral home. But the thing about Ka-chan was that she wanted to be an anthropologist, which is someone who studies human beings, and you have to go to grad school in order to learn how to do that. That's how the Deal was born, and the Deal was that when the time was right, Ka-chan would get to go to grad school and the whole family would go along to keep her company.

So now the time was right, at least for Ka-chan and Mugsy. For Jess, the time would never be right to leave the Northeast Kingdom. Even now, when they were on the Eve of Departure, she couldn't believe how the Deal had managed to sneak up on her. One minute she was helping her friend Litka choose a lamb to raise for 4-H, and the next Ka-chan was screaming and whooping and hopping all around because a letter had come from the grad school she liked best saying she could come study there. One minute Jess and Litka and their two other friends from the Green Mountain cohousing development, Zack and Dre, had been negotiating with the cohousing carpenters to get some leftover boards for their tree house addition, and the next Mugsy and Ka-chan had rented a moving van.

"Can't we leave in the fall?" Jess had asked, but even as the words were coming out of her mouth, she knew she wouldn't be ready to leave then, either. How could she stand to miss harvesting pumpkins and apples at Marty and

Lulu's Far Out Orchard and Farm, or helping plan the annual haunted house with Morrisville's volunteer firefighters? No time would be a good time to leave Vermont.

half-page

They had to leave now, her moms explained, so they could get settled into their new house in Arlington, MA, and so Ka-chan could go to the summer session of grad school. There wasn't even a little bit of wiggle room, Jess could tell. They would be gone before the end of mud season, and before their neighbor Elliot showed up to take Jess brook trout fishing, one of her most favorite things on earth.

"Uncle Marc and Aunt Renee are going to live in Holy Smoke and take care of it for us," said Mugsy, her forehead all crinkled up as she tried to catch Jess's eye. "Doesn't that make you feel better, that it's still going to be in the family?"

Jess shrugged. Her aunt and uncle would just

3

put their weird brand of decoration on her house, and how may times did she have to say that she didn't want to leave? One time when she was saying it, Ka-chan had started to cry and ran out of the room, which was extremely awful because Ka-chan never cried. Then Mugsy was very firm with Jess and told her to think about someone other than herself for once. Then later, Jess overheard Ka-chan telling Mugsy, "She's seven! She's supposed to be selfish!"

Jess didn't exactly want to be selfish, but she had still been hoping that there could be a way around the Deal. She and Litka and Zack and Dre had done a lot of planning about it. They all had good imaginations—Mugsy said that this was because they were homeschoolers and were allowed to be their own people in the world—but even with as many good ideas as they came up with, Jess had a sinking feeling that nothing was going to work. She had a sinking feeling that the grown-ups were going to win on this one. Sure enough, despite everything Jess said, despite all of her and Dre and Litka and Zack's scheming, the E-P-s were hitting the road tomorrow, "At the crack of dawn!" Ka-chan kept reminding everyone. They were driving all the way to Arlington, MA. All of them except Oni.

Oni was Jess's dog. He was five years old and

was half Australian cow dog and half shepherd. He had big, wide-set eyes and sticky-up black ears that drooped at the tips and were really soft. His tail was big and feathery and very proud. Also, he had the most original fur: black and white patches and then these fuzzy, orange-y spots that looked like pebbles on the bottom of a stream. He and Jess had grown up together.

"Oni would be miserable in Arlington, MA," Mugsy had told Jess when she broke the news that Oni wouldn't be coming with them. "He'll be a lot happier here with Marty and Lulu."

That was because in Vermont, Oni could go outside whenever he wanted, patrol around and go into the woods, get a lot of exercise and have his own life. But dogs in the suburbs—that's what Arlington, MA, was, a suburb—had to be on leashes, and Oni had never been on a leash in his life. He would hate it, said Mugsy. Marty and Lulu already had two of Oni's siblings, Nip and Tuck, who kept the sheep on their farm in order. Oni went over to work with them a lot, too, and Lulu had been teaching Jess how to run him. Mugsy said Oni could get on with his life at the Far Out Orchard and Farm.

"In Arlington, MA, Oni wouldn't be able to be his own person," Mugsy said. Jess wanted to know who would ever want to live in a stupid place where a dog couldn't even be his own person?

On the Eve of Departure, Oni didn't go off for his afternoon woods patrol. He stuck close to Jess and kept butting her hand whenever she stopped scritchling his ears. He walked with her to the tree house, where she was going to sleep that night, and stayed next to the trunk waiting for her to come back down while she hauled up her sleeping bag. She could never get him to climb up there with her, and if she tried to carry him, he squirmed and kicked and howled until she just gave up. He must be afraid of heights, said Ka-chan. It was just one of the things about him that made him who he was, like how he insisted on going out at night to check on things, and how he made it clear to everyone that the only place he was ever going to sleep was on his mat in the kitchen by the wood stove.

Probably there weren't any tree houses in the suburb of Arlington, MA. And no tree house could be this good, anyway. It had belonged to Mugsy and Marc when they were kids, but it was even older than that, because someone else—Jess wasn't sure who—had started it way back in the past. Like lots of regular houses around Morrisville, the tree house had been improved on in various ways. For one thing, it had two stories. The first story you got to by climbing up slats nailed to the tree trunk, and it was big enough for four kids if you squished. The second story was more of a lookout. The third story—the one they were supposed to build this summer—was going to be really fancy and cool, but now Jess wasn't going to be able to work on it at all. Oni whined at her from below and she hurried down to be with him. She didn't want to waste a moment.

That night, the E-Ps went to the Joint for pizza because Mugsy and Ka-chan were too tired to cook and anyway, all the pots and pans had been packed. The twins took over the whole place, as usual, running around and saying hi to everyone at the other tables. Meena and Rem, who owned the Joint, had made the mistake one time of letting the boys get their own sodas from the soda machine, and now Cam and Hank were obsessed with wanting to pull the levers. They were running around, running around, with Ka-chan and Mugsy running around after them, and Jess just sat in the booth eating leftover pizza crusts and wishing Oni could have come to eat out with them, but he wasn't allowed in the Joint.

Suddenly, the doors banged open and all kinds of people crowded in. There was Eddie, the minister from church, Uncle Marc and Aunt Renee and Uncle Lurvy and a bunch of other grown-ups who were friends and neighbors, like Marty and

Lulu and Sam-man and Sam-woman and Wesley from the co-op, Elliot, Litka's mom and Litka, Zack and his dad Leonard, Ella and Nia and all those folks from cohousing and all the kids who came with them—including Dre and a lot of other people who had been helping them load the van but who had gone home to get their own suppers, or at least that's what they'd said. "See you in the morning!" they'd said, but now here they were back again.

"Surprise!" people were shouting, and "Bon voyage! Good luck! We'll miss you!"

Sam-woman was taking bottles of fizzy cider out of a bag and opening them with loud pops. Meena cleared off a table for all the desserts people had brought, and the folks who'd been eating at the Joint either paid their bill and left or joined the party.

"Did you think any more about our plan?" Dre asked Jess quietly, sliding into the booth beside her. Zack and Litka slid in, too, watching her anxiously. After all their work, the best thing they could come up with was for Jess to slip away in the confusion the next morning, hide in the woods, then stay holed up in the tree house for a while. They had been getting things ready for the past couple of weeks, and there were two big plastic containers of food up there, mostly cans of soup and beans. It wasn't safe to leave better food like crackers or cookies because critters would get it, even in a plastic container.

When Jess thought about it one way, she loved the idea of living in the tree house, hiding out from everyone, depending on her excellent knowledge of outdoor skills, depending on her wits and the help of her good friends to stay in the place she belonged. When she thought about it another way, though, she suspected she would be lonely, cold and probably scared out in the woods all by herself for that long. Litka and Zack and Dre would have to sneak around to come and see her and keep a really big secret. Looking at her friends' faces as they sat with her in the booth, she could tell they were feeling pretty hopeless as well.

"What if you fake like you're really sick and can't be moved for fear you'll die?" This was Litka's plan, and it had actually worked for her a couple of times when she didn't want to go visit her mean cousins in New Hampshire. She had read in a book how to fake a fever by heating yourself up under the covers with a heating pad and then hiding the heating pad.

"The heating pad's already packed," said Jess. "And it only works when they don't take your temperature with a thermometer, but Mugsy always does."

Litka nodded sadly. Her mom never bothered to do more than use her cheek or the back of her hand to check on a fever. They'd already had this conversation a few hundred times.

Zack opened his mouth to start on his favorite plan, the one about getting his dad to adopt Jess because Jess and Leonard were good friends already, but that was even more unlikely than the sick plan or the tree house plan. Just then, the grownups started singing, "For they're a jolly good family!" and Zack shut his mouth. The whole time everyone was singing, Dre just scooched closer and closer to Jess until she was smushed up against the wall, but she didn't push him back or anything. It was like how Oni sometimes leaned against her legs, hard. She knew Dre, who was a very shy and quiet person, was just giving her a hug goodbye.

CHAPTER TWO:
THE FARM WITH THE SKYLINE

Moving Day had been very long. Mugsy drove the moving van and Ka-chan drove their car, and they drove and drove and drove. The whole awful day had started off with saying goodbye to Oni. When he realized he wasn't going with them, his ears had gone flat and his tail had stopped wagging and he'd barked and barked as they drove off. Lulu was holding his collar and Jess could tell Oni was pulling his hardest to get away from her and run after the car. It had been the most horrible thing in her life so far, and Jess hated thinking about it, so she just tried to stay asleep. That wasn't so easy, since her brothers never slept in the car. They always sang and shouted and fought, and Moving Day was no different, with the extra added part that the boys both wanted to ride in the moving van with Mugsy but Ka-chan wouldn't allow it, so there was crying, as well. All in all, by the time they pulled up to the new house and everyone got out, Jess was in a terrible, sleepy, grumpy mood. Plus, the new house was nothing special. Way smaller than their real house, with just some square rooms and first and second floors. No nooks or crannies or secret staircases to the secret third floor; nothing interesting. As soon as they'd made a quick tour, Ka-chan looked at her watch and said, "The movers will be here in an hour or so to unload the van. We have time to go to the park!"

"Yes, kids, what do you think? We live near a wonderful park now!" said Mugsy, as if that would make up for having left the woods behind. "And we'll be able to see the Boston skyline!" Whatever that was. Jess was too grumpy to ask.

The park was basically a bunch of grass fields. The skyline was a far-away bunch of big, tall buildings, some of them with pointy antennae things on their tops.

"Boston is less than 10 miles from here," said Ka-chan dreamily, "but doesn't it look like those buildings are floating on a magical island far, far away?" You could tell she was already loving being in Arlington, MA, and was excited about leaving Vermont and starting grad school, and that made Jess so mad she felt like spitting. Jess thought the skyline just looked like dumb buildings. And what's more, a skyline is not the thing you want to look at when you'd rather see mountains and forest.

"They call it 'Skyline Park' because of this fabulous view," said Mugsy. She and Jess were standing on a bench right at the top of a hill while Ka-chan stood with the twins on the next bench over. The benches didn't seem all that clean, but Ka-chan made everyone take off their shoes anyway, and Jess's feet were getting cold. Taking off your shoes before you stood on something where people sat was one of the Japanese things Ka-chan did. There was no arguing with her, either. Mugsy rubbed one foot with the other, so her feet must be getting cold, too. "The information I got from the Arlington Chamber of Commerce said that this park used to be a farm," she said. "Robbins Farm."

"Really?" Jess thought a farm was a lot more interesting than a skyline. She started to wake up and feel just a smidge less grumpy. "Where's the barn?"

"There aren't any buildings left anymore. But if we go to the library to do a little research, I bet we can find some pictures."

Jess sighed. Mugsy was always going to the library to see what she could find out about things that the kids asked her. She was a librarian, and that's what librarians did, but usually by the time Mugsy'd found something out, Jess had forgotten why she'd been interested in the first place. Now that Mugsy was going to be working at the library again, right here in Arlington, MA, Jess figured there would be no way of stopping her. Probably they would all be mostly living at the library.

"Here we go, raisins! Here we go!" shouted Cam and then both he and Hank hopped off the bench and started rolling down the hill just as quickly as they could, with Ka-chan yelling at them to put on their shoes.

The next morning, Jess woke up early and decided to do some exploring in the park. Even though it wasn't the woods, it was still better than staying inside. She picked her way through the half-unpacked boxes that were strewn all over the new house, and went off to see what there was to see. She took her new pocket knife—an early birthday present—her bug collecting kit and her binos in case she had to see something far away or if there was an interesting bird. Outside, the air was cool and the sky was just starting to lighten up. Jess tried not to think about Oni, or rather, she thought about how much he would truly hate it here. Mugsy had sure been right about that. There were lots of sidewalks and streets with cars and too many houses and not enough trees. On the other hand, there were hundreds of squirrels, which he would certainly enjoy.

Jess remembered exactly how to get from the

new house to the "wonderful" park. She walked past a yard with lots of garden gnomes in it, turned onto a downwards-sloping road and immediately passed three dogs being walked. One: a really old pug whose eyes stuck out and were misted over, so maybe he was blind. His walker, an old white man in a business suit, smiled at her, but didn't stop to talk, which was fine with Jess. Two: a chocolate lab, wearing a knapsack for some reason. Jess stopped to take a closer look, and the blonde walker snapped, "Please don't pet her! She's training to be a service dog!" Jess hadn't been going to pet her, but she said, "Ok!" and tried to look like the lady hadn't hurt her feelings. Three: some kind of fluffy white-and-brown puppy, who flopped over at her feet, rolled around, then got up and peed in excitement, just missing her right shoe. The puppy's person, a boy about Jess's age, was embarrassed about this. His freckly cheeks turned red and he pulled the puppy away. The boy was a carrot top, with hair almost long enough to make into a ponytail.

"Sorry," he muttered, and made a clicking sound at the puppy, but the puppy ignored him and just kept trying to get back to Jess, wagging and whining. Then the puppy rolled right in her own pee, and both Jess and the boy said, "Eeeww!" together, starting to laugh.

15

"Puppies are wicked messy!" said the boy. "She's always rolling around in something gross, like a dead worm or poop!"

"I know!" said Jess. "Puppies are a lot of work."

"Do you have a dog?" the boy asked. He looked over at her from under his long bangs.

"Yes." Jess right away got sad, even with a big smile still on her face.

"Boy or girl?"

"Boy."

"Where is he?" All of a sudden, this guy was really asking a lot of questions.

"We had to leave him in Vermont. He's never walked on a leash."

"Oh." The boy finally got the puppy away from the pee puddle and clicked at her to walk along, but she ended up almost tearing his arm out because she saw another dog on the other side of the street and started running. The boy started running, too.

"Bye!" he shouted over his shoulder. "See ya!"

"See ya," Jess replied, kind of quietly. She was thinking about Oni, of course. She didn't remember him when he was as little as the boy's dog, because she was little herself at the time. She watched the boy run, with his little fluffball jumping all around on her leash. Jess sighed and kept going. She found the driveway that led to the park and turned in. It seemed a little weird that you had to go up someone's driveway, but Mugsy said that people who owned property abutting the park had to let people walk up their driveways to get there. "Abutting" meant touching and was a rather strange word. Even though she read a lot, Jess didn't think she'd come across that one before. Now that she knew it, though, she'd probably see it in the very next book she read, which would probably be *The Wolves of Willoughby Chase*. Ka-chan said there was nothing like your favorite adventure book to take your mind off your troubles, and if having to move to Arlington, MA, wasn't troubles, Jess didn't know what was.

Well, here she was in the park. She walked to the left, keeping to the perimeter. The skyline was red from the rising sun, shiny in the early morning light. Since she was already sad about Oni, the skyline didn't make her sad the way it did yesterday. It maybe even looked like a magical island. Sort of. Jess got up on a bench, neglecting to remove her shoes, and was staring at the skyline when she noticed something in her peripheral vision. Over there in the playground, at the bottom of the hill Cam and Hank had tumbled down, two people were slowly walking around. They were the only other people in the park, and she couldn't see the exact details, but they clearly had some kind of machines. They were sweeping the machines over the ground like vacuum cleaners.

Jess hopped off the bench and moved closer. There was nowhere to hide in the park, so she just pretended to be doing a little bird watching through her binos, and the people with machines didn't pay any attention to her. Sometimes being right out in the open was the best way to spy. As she got closer, she could hear a beeping coming from the machines. She stood quietly by the wooden playhouse to watch. The machines had a round thing that looked like a little steering wheel at the bottom, and a little screen near the top. The grownups each had one, and they were sweeping the steering wheel end over the dirt. All of a sudden, one of the machines started beeping like crazy. The person—an Asian guy who looked a little like her Uncle Kenny in Hawaii, with a big nose and long hair—got a gleam in his eye, and if he'd been a dog his ears would have perked up. He swooshed the machine over the ground again until he pinpointed the exact place that made the loudest beeping. Then he shut it off, grabbed a trowel out of his back pocket and started to dig.

"Got something, Stan?" The other person was a really tall white lady with short, bright red hair. She drifted over to Stan's side, peering down at the ground.

"Dunno," he said. "Machine was going wild. I could do without another batch of beaver pull tabs, though."

"Beaver pull tabs make life worth living!" the lady said, and the two of them chuckled. The man kept digging, carefully slicing up little chunks of dirt. He kept going and going. "It's a deep find, that's for sure," he muttered. He was kneeling and sticking his butt way up, the way Oni did when he found a chipmunk hole.

It seemed like the digging was taking forever, but then the man said, "Aha! I've got you!" and "Come to Daddy!" He pulled something out.

"What is it? What is it? Let me see!" The red-hair lady was jiggling from one foot to another. Jess caught her excitement, and her heart started to beat faster.

The man was still kneeling by the hole, brushing dirt off whatever it was, looking at it very carefully. Suddenly, he started rolling around on the ground, screaming out, "WOO HOO!" The lady yelled, "What? What? What?" as the man scrambled to his feet and started to dance. He shook his arms in the air, he shook his butt, he stamped and hollered and screamed out, "Yes! Yes! Yes!" He jumped up and down and then finally stopped long enough to show the lady what it was —Jess couldn't see, even though she'd moved quite a bit closer—and then the lady started screaming too. It was a whole screamfest in the early morning park! The man clutched whatever it was tightly in his fist, and the two of them ran all around, shouting like anything. Jess couldn't stand it anymore.

"What did you find?" Jess had to shout pretty loudly herself a couple of times for them to hear her and finally calm down enough to answer.

"Little girl," the man said in a very solemn voice and very out of breath. "Little girl! Here, in the early dawn hours of a beautiful spring day in Arlington, Massachusetts, you have been present at our most important find ever. You have been witness to the stunning and utterly monumental moment that Stan and Talia found ..." Then the two grownups looked right in each other's faces and screamed out together, "A PINE TREE SHILLING!"

"Get the camera, get the camera!" Stan said, and Talia ran over to an old jeep parked at the curb and came back with a camera.

put on p. 22?

"Do you know how to take pictures?" she asked Jess, and Jess did, from having taken a photography class with Dre one time.

"Ok, we're going to reenact the whole thing, ok? You be the camera person."

"Can I see it first?" Jess asked, so Stan held the coin out to her in his grubby hand, and even let her touch it, although he just couldn't bear to let her actually hold it. It did look very old, and very, very cool: a thin metal disk with the edges worn down, a scrubbly pine tree in the middle and old time letters that spelled out "MASATHVSETS" on one side and the date "1652" on the other side. It was the state coin of Massachusetts a really long time ago, Stan told her. "It's incredibly rare," he said.

"This coin is 356 years old!" said Talia, then she looked up at the sky and sang out, "Take me now, oh Lord!"

Stan laughed and nodded his head. "Yes, I think I can die happy now. Wait until the others hear about this!"

He carefully stowed the ancient coin away in a box in his pocket and had Jess take a bunch of pictures as he and Talia pretended to get the signal on the screen of their metal detector, then start digging, then the whole discovery, with lots of amazed and surprised expressions and gestures. Jess thought it looked really fake, but she didn't say anything. They were the most excited grown ups she'd ever met, and they assured her that this was something amazing she would be able to tell her grandchildren: The Time I Witnessed the Greatest Find of the Century So Far. Then they shared their celebratory breakfast of granola bars and orange juice with her.

Back at the new house, Mugsy and Ka-chan were sitting at the table drinking tea and the twins were still sleeping. Her moms looked up, surprised, when Jess came through the back door.

"Have you already been somewhere?" asked Mugsy, holding her arms out for a hug.

"Yes, to the park." Jess took off her shoes and tried to pretend she didn't see Mugsy's "come hug me" stance. Mugsy was a big hugger, and she would get fussy if you didn't give her a squeeze whenever she asked for one, even if you didn't really feel like getting all up close and personal. Mugsy didn't back down, so Jess sighed and got the hug over with quickly, then started rummaging around to find her own tea—the apple and cinnamon one that Litka's mom made and sold at the farmer's market. Even though she really wanted to tell her moms about the Pine Tree Shilling, she couldn't quite make herself do it. If she let them know she'd had a good time at the park—that she'd already had an actual adventure—they might start thinking that she was glad to be in Arlington, MA, and she was definitely not glad, not one little bit.

"When the boys wake up, we thought we'd check out the town and find a place to eat. I think they might have a diner," said Ka-chan. She and Mugsy were diner fiends. "Then I have to go over to grad school."

"Ok," said Jess, giving up on the tea, which she couldn't find anywhere. It was going to take forever to get organized in here.

"Looking for your tea?" said Mugsy. "Try that box under the window. I remember packing it." Sure enough, there it was. Jess's mug was even in there, the one that had been fired in the cohousing kiln when she and her friends had learned how to do pottery. Her mug had a fern pattern on one side and was nice and heavy. She sat down between her moms with her tea in front of her. Upstairs, they could hear the twins starting to wake up, which usually meant they had a twin fight in bed before they came out to see what everyone else was doing.

"Snickerdoodle pronto!" shouted Cam, and Hank growled back, "Mari-a-nate the ishkabibble!" which made Jess and her moms laugh. The guys picked up the weirdest words and used them for their own language. Jess listened to the familiar noise of the twin fight and closed her eyes, leaning into the fragrant apple-scented steam from her tea. It tasted better if you let it steep.

CHAPTER THREE:
BIGGER THAN PIKACHU

There were too many kids in Arlington, MA. You couldn't ever find a place to be alone, and everywhere you went, you could see that someone had been there before you, usually because they left some trash behind. Jess had found a few ok places at Robbins Farm, down behind bushes, in a little patch of scrub, or beside some rocks, but those places just weren't private. One time, she'd settled down in the scrub, digging around in the plant mulch to see if there were any interesting bugs. She was feeling lonely.

She missed her friends a lot, but not as much as she missed her dog. She missed Oni every minute, and she was missing him now. If he was here, he would pitch right in to help her dig. She also felt grumpy about not homeschooling this year, and had made sure to position herself so she couldn't see that stupid school over there across the field. Her moms were going to send her there. How could they send her to school? How many times had she heard Mugsy say proudly, "My daughter has never been to school a day in her life!"? "We're dyed-in-the-wool homeschoolers!" she'd say. Jess uncovered a worm and was experimenting with how fast it could dig itself back under, when two little kids, not much older than Hank and Cam, came blundering in. They were so excited to see her and so interested in the worm that she couldn't really be mad at them, but she gave their grownup an irritated glance as she exited the scrub. She remembered another time some kids her age were already in the scrub when she got there, and they threw twigs at her and yelled, "Don't come in our fort!" so she had to keep walking. You just couldn't find any peace and quiet around here.

Ka-chan had gotten busy right away getting ready for grad school, but that didn't mean she wasn't imposing order on the new house. She had everyone working to unpack boxes and finding new places to put all their stuff. Jess had a room and the twins had a room and there was a room in the basement without any windows that her moms said could be a rumpus room. The twins thought that meant they should dump out all their Lego and have a Lego rumpus, so Jess figured she'd better just keep her belongings upstairs in her room. Not that the boys might not get in there and rumpus, but it was a little safer. Her window looked across their driveway right into the next-door house, but the window over there always had a curtain over it. She'd never seen it open so far, and they had already been there two weeks. Her room was ok, not as nice as her real room in Holy Smoke, but ok. At least there was a good closet that you could walk into. Closets had been in short supply back home, because at the time Holy Smoke was built, most people didn't have as many clothes as folks do now, and the ones they did have, they kept in chiffarobes. That was a nice word to know.

Their third Saturday in Arlington, MA, Mugsy and Ka-chan called a family meeting. Back in Vermont, the E-Ps had family meetings at least once a week. The twins couldn't sit still for very long, especially Cam, so the moms always had Legos for them. This was going to be an important family meeting, Jess could tell, because the boys got a new Lego set. More *Star Wars*. Everyone sat around the dining table and, just like always, Mugsy started out asking if anyone had anything they wanted to bring up. Jess decided to wait, but Cam wondered about getting chickens, a rabbit, three cats and a guinea pig. Hank was paying more attention to putting together Flies on Skin (Twin Language for Qui-Gon Jinn), but he added that he liked blueberry pie. Jess watched Mugsy write, "Action Items: consider a pet; make pie." Mugsy looked up at Jess and raised her eyebrows, so Jess put in a request for Maggot Stew, a family favorite that was really just beef stew with orzo. Jess was starting small when, really, she had something big to ask.

Ka-chan told them that there was one more week to go before she started summer school. During that week, they were going to: go to Boston to the aquarium and the children's museum, go to Lexington to a museum about the Revolutionary War, explore the Minuteman Bike Trail again, visit their friends Dan and Ernesto in a town called Lowell, and have a tutor in for Jess to make sure she was going to be ready for second grade. Both moms looked at Jess after Ka-chan said this and, sure enough, this news made Jess want to argue.

"Why do I need a tutor?" she asked. "I can read and do math and tai chi and throw pots, fish and find fiddleheads. I'm probably smarter than these town kids in about 10 million ways."

"Well, you probably know some things that they don't, for sure," said Mugsy, taking a note. "But the school wants you to know the same things the other kids do, like what they already learned in first grade, and that's what the tutor is going to help you with. I'm sure it won't take very long, and she's really nice. I already talked with her and she's really looking forward to meeting you."

"You hired her and you didn't even ask me first?" Jess couldn't believe it. This wasn't how the E-Ps did things! "And, anyway, why can't we still homeschool?"

Ka-chan and Mugsy gave each other a look. That look made Jess really mad.

"I'm going to be in grad school," Ka-chan said in her patient-but-don't-push-me voice. "And Mugsy has her new job at Robbins Library, so no one will be home during the day. We need to do this for a while, Jess. You and me and the boys—we'll all do school for a while! And, baby, you're going to love this school. We've heard so many good things about it, and there are lots of kids who have two-mom families there, too."

Who cared about what kind of mom-family people had? School for her and preschool for the boys. Living in the suburbs. Jess had just about had it. Hank and Cam were getting enchanted with parks and toy stores and other stuff like that, but not Jess. The boys were actually getting swayed over to the side of starting to like it here. They were only little, but Jess was old enough to know what was important and real. Going into the woods with your dog, that was important.

Learning to whittle with your new pocketknife, that was real. Were they going to teach that in school? She hadn't told her moms because it wasn't any of their business, but yesterday she had tried to whittle a stick that must have been too green, because the blade slipped and nipped off just a tiny bit of the tip of one finger. It hardly even bled, and nobody noticed, but it made her wary of her new knife in a way she hadn't been before.

"School will be the death of me!" she wailed, which made the moms laugh and made her even angrier. She got so busy arguing about school and having a tutor that she forgot to bring up the other matter, at least until supper time.

The E-Ps had cleared their plates and were waiting for dessert. It was Saturday, so they were going to get something more treat-y than fruit and cheese. Hank and Cam were playing with their Lego creatures and making them talk in Twin Language. They were also making faces at each other across the table. There was no way they could sit next to each other without becoming what Mugsy said was "an extremely disruptive element to family dining."

"Abu-dangerous, clack, clack!" said Hank, and Cam did some of the clicky tongue noises back. Those tongue noises always made Mugsy laugh, but she was out of the room getting dessert. When she came back with a big bowl of tapioca pudding, everyone was quiet for a moment. Pudding was central in their family.

"When are we going to move back?" Jess asked quietly into her tapioca.

"What, baby?" asked Mugsy, patting the back of her spoon fondly onto the wiggly pudding. Jess asked her question again before Mugsy could get fully into her pudding reverie. Mugsy loved pudding so much that sometimes she sang a song about it.

"When are we moving back home?" Jess asked, more loudly.

Mugsy and Ka-chan looked another one of those grownup looks at each other. Jess didn't appreciate it. She knew there was a lot more going on in the grownup world than she could figure out. It was like life in a drop of water under the microscope. You couldn't see all those little creatures with the naked eye, but they were still there, wiggling around. Cam and Hank looked a twin look at each other then started spooning up pudding as fast as they could.

"Oh, honey," said Ka-chan. "We live in Arlington now. Arlington is our home."

"But what if I don't like it here in Arlington?" Jess asked. "What about that?"

Ka-chan put down her pudding spoon and

looked at the twins. "Boys, if you've finished your pudding, clear your places and scamper like bunnies upstairs. Brush your dentures and get on your pj's and I'm right behind you to read some *Mrs. Piggle-Wiggle*." All three of them left in a flurry of scraped-back chairs and rattling dishes. Jess just sat there. As much as she loved tapioca, it seemed like a lot of energy to pick up her spoon.

"Leave your pudding; I'll get it later," said Mugsy. "Come into the living room and let's talk."

This always happened! Ka-chan cleared off with the twins so Mugsy could do the explaining. Mugsy was good at explaining, but how could she explain this? Jess just wanted to go home.

In the living room, Mugsy shoved some Legos off the big, red, squishy armchair and snuggled Jess down on her lap. Mugsy was a very comfortable person, nice and soft. There was a lot of room on her. Jess rested her head on her mom's shoulder and closed her eyes. Mugsy smelled a little salty and a little like carnations, from her special soap that was French and that she spent a lot of money on because she said surely she was allowed this one small indulgence.

"Kitten Baby, sweetheart, I know you're not exactly loving it here." Mugsy stroked Jess's hair the way she always did, the way she had when Jess really was a Kitten Baby, just a little small girl pretending to be a cat, purring and kneading her mom's tummy with her paws. Jess's eyes filled up and she thought she was going to cry. She didn't cry much these days, and she didn't want to now. She knew it was complicated, and that's what Mugsy said next.

"It's complicated, Jess. We like Vermont, too. I love Vermont—I was born and raised there! And I know you're a true girl from the Queendom, aren't you, sweetie?" That's what her moms always joked, that they lived in the Northeast Queendom instead of the Northeast Kingdom. Jess nodded, still working on not filling up. Cam and Hank cried all the time about baby things like give-me-my-Thomas-engine-back and you-ripped-my-Pokémon-card, but this was not a baby thing. This was much, much bigger than Pikachu.

"You know how Cam and Hank think everything is about them?" asked Mugsy. Jess mmm-hmm-ed, but she already didn't like the direction this was heading in. "A family is like a big amoeba," Mugsy continued. "Sometimes one part puts out a pseudopod—like when you were born, you were a great big pseudopod and we all paid attention to you because you were just a baby; you needed us so much." Jess said mmm-hmm again and one tiny tear leaked out. "Then when the boys were born, they were big pseudopods;

33

even though yours was still important, you were more independent and out in the world on your own." Mugsy stopped to consider her explanation, shook her head a little, frowning, then continued. "Anyway, what I'm trying to say, Jess, is that right now it's Ka-chan's turn to put out her pseudopod. And the rest of us get to support her because she supported all of us for so long, like when she and I moved back to Morrisville and when she grew all you kids in her uterus and stayed home when I worked at the library and she cooked and took care of the house and you critters." Jess was starting to slip off Mugsy's lap so Mugsy heaved her back up. More tears were leaking out of Jess. She knew all of this already.

"Here's another thing," Mugsy said, clearing her throat. "Every person has dreams. I mean, every person actually has a job to do, and I don't just mean to earn money, even though that's important too. Ka-chan has been waiting a long time to add on to her job of being your mom and my wife. We're here in Arlington to help Ka-chan achieve her dream, because we love her, and it's her turn."

Mugsy went on to say a bunch of other things, mostly repeats of what she'd already said, and then she gave Jess a huge squeeze and said, "I know you're sad, Kitten Baby. But I'm counting on you. Plus, I have faith in you. I think you know how to make the best of this situation. I really do."

So they were staying. Jess had known that when she asked the question at supper; she had just been hoping, because she really, really hated it here. And things do change. Life is change; that's what Zack's dad, Leonard, said. It was a tai chi thing, but it made sense to Jess. So, ok. Ok. She would grin and bear it, take one for the team, make the best of things, and let Ka-chan put out her pseudopod. But whatever Mugsy kept saying about luck and "the good news is" and "home is where your family is," Jess would never be an Arlingtonian. Jess was, and always would be, a Vermonter to her core.

CHAPTER FOUR:
THE OLD GUY

Hank and Cam were having an Episode. This one had hair pulling and bad words and was set off by Cam finding Lego Luke Skywalker's sword thrown into the toilet bowl. What was worse, Cam didn't notice until he'd peed all over it. Oni hated Episodes, and if they'd been back home, he and Jess would have shared a look, grabbed a few provisions, and gone into the woods—maybe to the treehouse, maybe to some other destination. Here in Arlington, Jess was on her own. She slipped quietly out of the house and went to Robbins Farm.

It was early enough that there weren't very many people at the park. Jess got into the little patch of scrub and settled down to have some fruit leather. She saw a dog she liked, a scruffy little terrier whose name was Mrs. Beazley, but she didn't go say hi because she didn't feel like talking to Mrs. Beazley's person. After a while they left and Jess decided to go check on the playground.

Stan had told her several times that it was statistically astronomically improbable that there would be another Pine Tree Shilling find in the same place as their monumental discovery, but Talia had said, "A girl can dream, dude!" and Jess did dream about that shilling. A lot.

She decided to go look around at the bottom of the slides. Those slides were huge—built into the side of the hill—but they didn't go as fast as they looked. They didn't go fast at all, actually. You just sat there and slowly trickled down. Jess didn't understand how that was possible, but that's what happened. So far she hadn't found anything in the playground except a very beat up penny with a nick out of the side; old, but not as old as the Pine Tree Shilling.

As she came out of the scrub, she noticed someone over by the benches, way on the other side of the park. Sometimes people did tai chi over there, but this person wasn't doing moves. This person was bending down and picking things up. Jess used her binos and to take stock of the situation. It was an old guy with huge glasses, and he was picking things up off the ground and tossing them into the trash can. Cigarette butts, Jess thought. Now that she thought about it, Jess remembered she had seen quite a lot of cigarette butts sprinkled around on that hilltop. She put her binos away, took a drink from her canteen and, keeping to the perimeter, walked over there.

"So far, I've found 125. Can you believe it?" the old guy said when she came up to him. He didn't even look at her, just kept on with his collecting.

"Gross!" said Jess.

"I know! Why do they throw them on the ground?"

"They're pigs!" Jess decided to help him. Whenever Mugsy picked up trash in a public place, she and Ka-chan always had this conversation:

Ka-chan: God, people are pigs!

Mugsy: This piece of trash is unsightly. I think I'll pick it up so the next people who walk here won't have to look at it.

Ka-chan: God, people are pigs!

The cigarette butts were definitely unsightly, all squished up, some of them, others ragged and coming to pieces, some of them very fresh, even with lipstick on them. And if you got close enough, they smelled. They were everywhere, up one side of the hill and down the other.

"What's the deal with all of these?" Jess asked the old guy, dropping a handful into the trash.

"People like to come out here and smoke and look at the skyline," he said. "137."

"I got 15 so far," said Jess.

"Well, keep track of how many you get, and we'll add them together at the end."

"Do you smoke?" Jess asked. She knew plenty of people in Vermont who did, and even Mugsy used to when she was in college before she met Ka-chan. "Ka-chan very wisely said she wouldn't keep dating me unless I went Cold Turkey," Mugsy would say, then both she and Ka-chan would start singing, "Cold Turkey," which was a song by John Lennon, who was one of the Beatles, but it wasn't a Beatles song. Jess didn't know why quitting smoking cigarettes was called Cold Turkey, but she was glad Mugsy didn't smoke anymore since it wasn't good for you and could make you sick.

Litka's mom smoked, but she always went outside the house to do it and looked guilty if you noticed. Jess secretly kind of liked the way it smelled, or maybe she just liked the way Litka's mom smelled, smoky and friendly and like a kind of perfume called Marvelous that she kept on her dresser.

"I used to smoke when I was younger—pretty much everyone did back then," said the old guy. "142. But my first wife said she would kick me out if I didn't stop, so I stopped."

"Did you go Cold Turkey?" asked Jess. "27."

"Yes. I had to chew a lot of gum and it gave me a headache, but I had to do something instead of smoking. 150."

"My mom said she used a patch," said Jess. "Don't you think that's weird? A patch?"

"165. Pick up the pace. I have to go soon, and I want to get to at least 300."

By the time the old guy left, saying, "Keep working!" and going off fast on his long legs, they had picked up 292 butts and that was really scraping the bottom of the barrel, and sometimes even doing some excavation to get really old ones out of the ground. The whole area around the benches looked sparkly clean now, because they had picked up all the other little bits of trash, too: the bottle caps and the candy wrappers and the chewed up gum. They hadn't found any money, though, which seemed strange. Maybe Stan and Talia had already been through.

"Eight more, eight more," Jess muttered, swinging out in wider and wider circles. There had to be some more around, and sure enough, with just a little digging, she managed to find them.

"I did it!" she yelled, and a big kid who was going over to play basketball with his friends yelled, "Good for you, midget!" and his friends laughed.

Jess turned her back on them. How could she let the old guy know that they'd made 300? She didn't know where he lived, and she certainly didn't have his phone number. They had just been working together to get the job done. She tossed the last butts into the trash can, trying not to breathe the nasty smell of poop bags mixed with stale tobacco. She scanned the area, trying to think how she could get a message to her fellow cleaner-upper. The three benches were on a slab of concrete, in a semi-circle, looking out toward the skyline. The trash can was bolted to the concrete, too. Concrete. Like a sidewalk! You could write on it, Jess realized, with sidewalk chalk.

When Jess came pelting into the house, Mugsy hollered, "Jess! Where have you been? We're getting ready to go to church!"

"Just a minute! I'll be right back!"

"15 minutes, Jess! Synchronize your watch!"

Jess nodded, then pelted into the garage and grabbed the bucket of sidewalk chalk that was hanging around in there. Back at the benches, she ignored a couple of grownups who were cuddling, and wrote in tall letters:

300 CIGERET BUTS PIKD UP HEER! GROS! DONOT LITER! DONOT BE UNSITLY!

Then she drew a picture of a cigarette butt in a circle and put a line through it. There. Now the old guy would know that they had fulfilled their quota, and so would everybody else. And maybe they wouldn't be such pigs from now on.

"Stay there!" Ka-chan ordered when Jess came screeching to a halt in their driveway, after having run like a banshee all the way from the park. Ka-chan took the bucket of chalk from her and put it on the porch, then brushed and patted the chalk dust from her jeans. "Your hair," she said, and went to lick her fingers so she could smooth it, but Jess ducked away and escaped into the car, where her brothers were already in their booster seats.

"I'm going to touch you with the toilet sword!" hollered Cam, waving it at her.

"So what?" Jess said. Toilet water, even pee water, was nothing compared to cigarette butt grossness. Come to think of it, it would probably be good to wash her hands because they really smelled at this point. There would be a bathroom at church, she guessed, but until then she'd try to keep them out of range of Mugsy's sensitive nose.

"Told you so, itty bitty po," Hank said to his twin, and they went off into some of their Twin Language. Sometimes it made Jess laugh, and other times it was just annoying. Right now it was annoying. She was thinking she would probably hate church.

The new church was the same brand as their old one, UU, but was really big and there were a lot of people and they were all a little too friendly. As soon as the E-Ps walked through the door, a bunch of grownups started crowding them, making them write their names on stickers to stick to their shirts, and another lady came and introduced herself to Jess and the twins and said about how there was going to be RE today and please come to class and be welcome and Jess thought: ok, no way.

She looked up at her moms to telegraph to them that they better not try and make her, but they were smiling at each other and looking all around and they had really big happy expressions on their faces. When they sat down, two grownups started talking to them right away about welcome and Arlington schools are great and we feel very welcome here and there are lots of two-mom families and it's so wonderful. And welcome.

Church was long, and after a thing where all the kids went to sit at the front and someone told a story—Jess stayed where she was, but the twins were all over it—the kids were supposed to go to their RE. Back home, this would be when Jess and her friends would go out back to the yurt where they painted and sang, but Jess doubted city RE would be anywhere near as interesting. Ka-chan went with the twins, who were revved up like all get out. Jess leaned against Mugsy, who put an arm around her, which looked friendly, but Jess could tell that Mugsy wished she'd gone to RE, too. People lined up to light candles and talk about their problems, the choir sang, and Jess felt sleepy. Then, out of the corner of her eye, she saw someone she knew coming in late and sitting at the edge of a row, right in her line of sight. The old guy! He was wearing the same clothes from before and it didn't look like anyone had smoothed down his hair, either.

Ushers passed around baskets of money, and when the one for his row got to the old guy, he put in some money and rummaged around and took out some other money, like he was making change for himself at a store. The lady with white hair sitting next to him gave him a nudge, but he just kept rummaging around until he'd found what he wanted.

44

Jess didn't listen to much of the sermon because she was keeping an eye on the old guy. He was interesting to watch because, like Cam, he couldn't sit still. He squirmed around and took something out of his pocket, looked at it, then put it back in. Jess wasn't sure, but thought it could have been a cigarette butt. 301! The old guy scratched his head and took off his glasses, polished them on his shirt, then put them back on and picked up the hymn book. He flipped through it, put it back down, took the thing out of his pocket again and then put it back. Then the lady next to him nudged him again, and he settled down, leaning back in the seat and looking up at the ceiling. Jess looked, too: nothing up there.

When she looked back at the old guy, his head had dropped all the way back, his mouth was open, and she could tell he was asleep. Either that or dead, but probably not dead or the lady sitting next to him would have noticed. Ka-chan came back and sat down on Jess's other side, nodding to Mugsy, who looked a question to her. So the twins had decided RE was cool. After that, Jess might have taken a little snooze herself, snug between her two moms. When she woke up, it was because Mugsy was bumping her as she rummaged in her pocket for a tissue. It must be the sermon, because that usually made Mugsy cry. Mugsy was something of a crier. Jess settled back against her mom, who was blowing her nose softly.

The minister said something about riding a bike and that made Jess wish she was riding on the dirt roads back in Vermont with her friends. You could really go places, unlike on the Minuteman Bike Trail, which, like everything else around here, was really crowded. Where did all these people come from? Little kids and people with baby strollers and joggers and skateboarders and scooter-ers. It was hard to get up a good head of steam in such a crowd.

Mugsy blew her nose again, gave a big sigh, then she and Ka-chan and Jess shared a hymnal and sang together. On the way out, Mugsy went to get the boys and Ka-chan made Jess stand in line so they could say thank you to the minister. Ka-chan even gave the minister a hug. Jess saw the old guy blow by the line of people waiting behind them and go straight to a table where there was a plate of brownies. Jess wriggled out of Ka-chan's grasp and went shyly over to say hi.

"They stopped having food at coffee hour," he said. "I think these are left over from some meeting. Better get one now."

"Do they have nuts?" asked Jess, and the old guy shook his head, so she took one. Nuts were fine on their own, but please don't put them in a brownie.

"Oh, I saw what you wrote," the old guy said. There was chocolate on his teeth. "And look, I have one in here for some reason." Sure enough, it had been a cigarette butt he'd been looking at in church. He took it out of his pocket and looked around for a trash can, then set it on the table next to the brownies. Jess giggled. Someone tapped the old guy on the shoulder and he turned around. Jess saw Mugsy and the boys and made her way through all the people to get to them. Some people said hi to her and she said hi back as politely as she could, but she didn't want to talk with anyone new.

"Let's go!" she said to Mugsy, who was famous for staying at church forever to talk to people, even when it was just the much smaller number of people who went to their church in Morrisville.

Mugsy looked at her and nodded, even though Jess could tell she wanted to stay. "Let's go! Let's go!" Jess said for good measure, and to her relief, Mugsy sent Cam over to get Ka-chan, who had just finished talking to the minister and some other people, and soon enough the E-Ps were in the car. Right away, Mugsy started sniffing.

"I've been smelling cigarettes all morning," she said, wrinkling up her nose. "Can anyone else smell cigarettes?"

CHAPTER FIVE:
FROWNIE FACE

The first Jess knew about it, she saw a sheet of paper stuck up on a tree in the park. "Have you seen this dog?" the paper asked, and there was a picture of a big, grumpy yellow dog. "Frownie Face has been missing for three days. Last seen in Robbins Farm Park wearing a purple collar. This is a special dog who came all the way from Tennessee and we miss her very much. Reward!"

Jess read the paper carefully several times. Frownie Face. So that was the dog's name. Because Jess *had* seen her, more than once. The only time Jess could get some peace and quiet was very early in the morning, so she had trained herself to wake up at 5 a.m. It was easy: you just lie in bed before you fall asleep and say, "5 a.m., 5 a.m., 5 a.m.!" very sternly to yourself, and then that's when you wake up. She had a stash of senbei crackers and fruit leather in her room for first breakfast, and she took a knapsack with her canteen, maybe her bug collecting kit if she felt

48

like it, and the book she was reading. Her knife was on her belt, of course.

She would go over to the park, the closest nature she could find, and roam around. There could be interesting stuff, if you looked hard enough. If you made the best of things. There was a whole fence covered with honeysuckle, for instance, and she loved sucking out the sweet nectar from the flowers. Twice now, she had been in the scrub, reading, and had sensed that there was an animal. When she looked up, she'd seen that same grumpy yellow dog loping along, the tags on her purple collar jingling. The dog had a guilty/excited look on her face, like she was getting away with something. Jess figured someone must let her out early to get some exercise before too many people were around, but now she realized that the dog was an escapee. An escapee from Tennessee.

"Where's Tennessee?" Jess asked Mugsy, who was scraping something off the kitchen floor with a butter knife. It was a risk to ask, but she took it. Back in the homeschooling days, Mugsy would have dropped everything and gotten out the atlas and a million other books and given Jess a whole lesson, but these days, things were different. "Down south," said Mugsy, barely looking up. "You know where the atlas is."

Jess knew where the atlas was in Holy Smoke —in the hutch in the second dining room, the one grownups didn't go into very often, so it was very kid friendly—but she had to think for a minute to remember where it was in the no-name Arlington house. In the living room, in a bookshelf next to the fireplace. Tennessee was a skinny, Lego block kind of a state, socked in by other Lego blocks like Kentucky, Mississippi and Alabama. Jess couldn't tell from looking at the map what made Tennessee a place for a special dog like Frownie Face to come from, just like she couldn't tell from the paper in the park what made Frownie Face so special to begin with. She looked like an ordinary yellow dog to Jess.

There was a new notebook on the coffee table in the living room. It had a picture of a kitten on it, and had been sitting there for a couple of days. Mugsy said it was for Jess to practice her writing in. Practicing writing was something that Teresa the Tutor wanted her to do. Teresa was a lot older than Jess's moms, had long gray hair and smelled like patchouli, like a lot of women at cohousing. "Dirt perfume," Mugsy called it. So Ms. Dirt Perfume Teresa wanted Jess to practice writing because she said the kids in second grade would be ahead of her.

After Teresa said that, she tried to make Jess

feel better by telling her that her reading level was more advanced "by a *great deal*" than most second graders. Jess hadn't even looked at the kitten notebook since Mugsy showed it to her, but now she snatched it up and took it to her room. Closing the door, she sat down on her bed, took a green marker and wrote in perfectly fine-looking letters:

Cach Frowny Fas. Clame rward.

Then she listed all the things she needed to do to capture the Escapee from Tennessee.

The next morning at 5:10 a.m., Jess was sitting in the scrub keeping a close watch on her Frownie Face trap. She had bought a new leash from a store on Mass Ave. where a lot of dogs had doggy day care. It had taken almost all of her savings. She also put a bowl filled with bread and cereal under a bush near the entrance of the park where she had seen the dog before. Meat would be better, but she hadn't been able to get any. She figured the dog was probably hungry enough to eat anything and, anyway, Oni loved bread and cereal and Jess thought Frownie Face would, too. A squirrel skittered down a tree trunk and got really close to the bowl. It stood up on its hind legs, sniffing. Darn! Jess was getting ready to go shoo it away, when she heard a jingling. She froze, then turned slowly toward the sound.

Frownie Face was coming at a fast trot, hugging the chain link fence, keeping an eye out. Any thoughts Jess had about just getting up and calling to the dog vanished. This was an animal who wasn't going to give up her freedom easily. There was something wild and wily about Frownie Face, something that said, "I'm on my own and I like it that way!" She'd even have to scrap her Plan B, Jess realized, which was to approach Frownie Face as she ate the bread and cereal, speaking softly and holding out another piece of bread, then quickly clipping the leash to her collar.

As Frownie Face came closer to the bowl, the squirrel dashed for a tree trunk, scolding and chattering. Frownie Face paused, her ears up. She sniffed all around, then slowly snuck up on the food and started gobbling. The whole time she was eating, she kept her ears up, so Jess didn't dare move. Frownie Face's tags hit the edge of the bowl making a soft clinking sound, and then the dog was on her way again, going purposefully along the fence, licking her lips.

When Jess slowly moved out of the scrub to try and follow her, the dog didn't even look back, just swiveled her ears and picked up the pace. Jess tried, but she couldn't keep up. She stopped running and stood watching as Frownie Face loped out of the park and down Eastern Ave. It was going to take a lot more than a few cornflakes and a new leash to complete this mission.

That Saturday, Jess came home after an unsuccessful early morning wait for Frownie Face, who had never showed.

"Where have you been?" asked Mugsy, serving her Mickey Mouse—shaped pancakes with some of the maple syrup they'd made last year. "The convoy will be here soon!" Then she started singing a song about a big ol' convoy and dancing around the room. Mugsy, Mugsy. But Jess started to smile as she ate. She had almost forgotten that today was the day a bunch of their friends from Morrisville were coming to visit. Dre, Litka and Zack were coming with their families, and some other grownups from cohousing. Lulu and Marty couldn't leave the farm because there was so much summer work to do in the fields. They had sent some pictures of Oni, though, herding sheep with Nip and Tuck, and they had been really good at sending the Oni report at least once a week.

The last one had started off, "Oni misses all of you and especially Jess," like it always did, and had gone on to say, "but he is working hard to learn all the things Nip and Tuck can teach him about herding, and he is doing a really good job. So when Nip has her puppies and needs to take a break, we think Oni will be able to substitute for her. He's getting *so much* exercise, and he's *such* a good boy!" They always wrote that at the end of the Oni report.

Missing Oni was something Jess felt all the time, and it was somehow different from the way she missed her friends. With Oni, she could feel how much she missed him, right in her body. She was always remembering things about him, like how he snuffled in her ears because he loved the taste of earwax: he would stick his slobbery tongue right in there if she let him, and sometimes she did.

Or how he would sometimes come home covered in hitchhikers and she would have to comb the stickery little burrs out of his belly fur, which tugged and must have hurt, but the only thing he would do was sigh or yawn or gently put his paw on her arm and look at her like, "Are we done here?" Or how he would lean against her legs until she was almost tipping over, wanting her to thump and thump and thump him.

"They're here! They're here!" the twins were shouting, so Jess got up from where she was lying on the couch rereading *Nightbirds on Nantucket* and went out with the rest of her family. Two cars pulled up and people started jumping out and running over for hugs. Jess watched until the cars were empty, even though she knew Oni was back on Marty and Lulu's farm. It was possible that someone had changed their mind and gone and gotten him. He wouldn't like it here to live, but he could visit, couldn't he? Litka, Zack and Dre were crowding around her, holding things like canned tomatoes and the blueberry jam Litka's mom made and a bunch of wilted basil from the cohousing garden. Jess felt shy with them at first, but then Litka said, "Come on and show us what's good around here!" Jess took them upstairs to see her room, and then they all went over to the park.

"Could be ok for sledding," said Zack, looking at the steeper hill, and then she was rolling and the rest of them were rolling after her. They rolled until they started to feel sick, then Jess took them back to the entrance where there was the paper about Frownie Face. The days-missing part had been changed to one week. She told them about her plan to capture the Escapee and secure the reward. Two more times, the dog had eaten bread and cereal, and two more times Jess had not been able to get near her.

"I don't think Frownie Face wants to go back to that family," she said. "She seems pretty happy just being out here on her own."

"What are you going to do with the money?" asked Zack. "How much do you think it is?"

Jess shrugged. She had thought a lot about what to do with the money, and most of her ideas were about going back to Vermont. She'd even considered running away—taking a bus, or just finding her way back to Holy Smoke, surviving on her own, outwitting the forces of evil. Except that Ka-chan and Mugsy weren't the forces of evil and she would miss them and they would be worried. As much as she wanted to believe she could, she knew that she couldn't leave Arlington on her own.

"You could buy some candy," said Litka. The last time Jess and Litka had talked on the phone, Jess had told her about an unbelievable candy store the E-Ps had found when they were exploring on their bikes. There was every kind of candy you could imagine in there. Candy lips, candy berries, candy worms, candy string and even candy Lego. The boys could hardly believe it. Ka-chan hated for the kids to eat sweet things—she made an exception for pudding—but even she was so amazed that she let everybody have a small bag. That's how it worked in the candy store: you went around with your bag and put different candies in.

"Would you have to give half to charity?" asked Dre. That's how it worked it his family: whenever he or any of his brothers or sisters got any money, they had to give half of it to charity. He usually gave his to the volunteer firefighters fund, which was a good cause, but Litka and Jess secretly agreed that if they had to give their money, they would give it to the animal shelter where Litka had adopted her dog, Mason, and her cats, Toad and Fig. The girls had volunteered at the shelter, and they would have done just about anything to get all of those sweet animals a home.

"I think I could keep it all," she said, "but I don't know how much it is."

"Probably around $100," said Zack.

"Maybe." 100 was the number Jess had dreamed about and it was exciting to hear Zack say it out loud. "I mean, that's a lot, but she's a big dog."

"Yeah, and you can tell they really love her," said Litka. "See how it says she's special?"

Weirdly, Frownie Face was a topic of conversation at the big backyard grill-out the E-Ps and their friends from Morrisville had that afternoon. The twins and the other littles were running around; grownups were sitting on folding chairs and chairs brought out from the dining room, filling up the backyard with their laughter and talk.

"I heard at church that the animal officer has seen that dog several times, but he hasn't been able to catch her," said Mugsy. Jess wasn't sure what an animal officer was, but probably the police for creatures. She was kind of glad that the creature police couldn't catch Frownie Face. Frownie Face was too smart for the creature police!

"I've been looking for her, too," she found herself bragging. She felt much more herself surrounded by her friends and neighbors from home. "I've been tracking her."

Zack's dad laughed his big laugh and slapped her five. "That's my Jess!" he said. "Sometimes it takes a smart girl to do a man's job!" Everybody laughed. "Seriously, though," he said, "tell me more about this dog." The two of them went to a more private area in the backyard and Jess told him about how she'd been feeding Frownie Face early in the morning.

"That's a really good idea," said Leonard. "She's not a wild creature, so she isn't used to being out on her own."

"She sure seems to like it, though," said Jess. "I think maybe she's thinking she *is* a wild creature now."

"Probably she is, at least a little bit," agreed Leonard. "But she's still got tame creature memories. I think you're on the right track, offering her food. And I think she might be lonely for being part of a pack by now. A human pack. I have a good feeling about you being able to rescue this dog, Jess. Keep me updated, ok?"

"Ok!" Jess felt more excited about the mission than ever. Leonard was a little bit psychic, which meant that he sometimes knew what was going to happen in the future or where to find something that had gotten lost. One time, he'd told Jess to look in her sock drawer for the ten-dollar bill she'd gotten for her birthday and had lost and was scared to tell her moms about and, sure enough, there it was. Jess thought that being psychic maybe came from doing so much tai chi.

"And remember ...," Leonard said. Jess joined him saying what he always said after they'd been doing tai chi, "Loose is longevity!" Which was a tai chi way of saying, "Take it easy," as far as Jess could tell.

Everyone was sad when their friends packed up and drove off in their convoy that evening. "We'd better do something to take our minds off missing everybody," said Ka-chan, so they went out to a little Japanese restaurant that Ka-chan said was halfway decent. In Morrisville, there hadn't been any Japanese restaurants, but there were lots around here. For Jess's birthday a week ago, they had gone to a really fancy one in Boston. The big discovery there was that every member of the E-P family adored sushi.

"Ebi, ebi, pumpkin pie!" sang Cam as they

waited for their tempura udon and kappa maki and miso soup and wakame salad. It wasn't easy, but Jess managed to wrap half a tempura ebi in a napkin and stash it in her pocket. The deep-fried shrimp made a terrible grease stain that she found later, but it was worth it. Tempura ebi turned out to be the best bait possible.

It was closer to 4:30 in the morning than 5:00 when Jess walked to the park. She was carrying the bowl with the ebi in it, the leash and her own hairbrush. She wasn't sure about the hairbrush, but even though Oni didn't like getting hitchhikers combed out of his fur, he loved being brushed, and she wondered if Frownie Face might like it too. She was just trying to cover a lot of bases.

She put the bowl with the ebi in it right where she always put the cornflakes and bread, and then, instead of going all the way over to the scrub, she sat very quietly and calmly on a rock that was right next to the bowl. For a long time, she sat there, a little chilly in the early morning air. She watched robins patrolling the field of grass and squirrels shaking their tails and making a racket as they rushed from tree to tree. A family of cardinals chip-chip-chipped as the parents worked on feeding their fledglings. She didn't know how long she'd been there when she finally heard the jingling of tags and knew that Frownie Face had decided to patrol the park this morning. The jingling came closer, then slowed. Jess could tell Frownie Face was very near. She could hear the dog sniffing.

"Does that ebi smell good, girl?" she asked softly, then, very, very carefully, she turned around. When Jess moved, Frownie Face stepped backward a few steps.

"Aren't you hungry?" asked Jess in a nice, sweet voice. It was the voice she used when she was full of love for Oni, when the two of them were just hanging out doing stuff together. Frownie Face sat down and her tail gave one feeble wag. Her ears went up and then down again, and she made a tiny whine. She sniffed toward the bowl and looked right at Jess.

"That's right," said Jess in her lovey voice. "You go ahead. You're a good, good girl. Aren't you a good girl? Aren't you a hungry girl? That food is for you, Frownie Face."

When she heard her name, Frownie Face whined again and wagged her tail for real. Jess smiled. She wanted to get up and pet the dog, but she had a feeling it was way too soon. "Loose is longevity," she whispered. "Stay loose."

For a long time, Jess talked to Frownie Face. She told her she was a special girl. She told her her family missed her and wanted her to come home. She told her that she, Jess, was her friend, and that she was going to help her get home before it got too cold to live outside. She told her that she'd had a big adventure but now it was time for the adventure to be over. Jess didn't know if Frownie Face's people had kids, but she told Frownie Face that her family was sad and missed her and that the kids were crying every night because they were worried about her. She told Frownie Face that it was her duty to give herself up and go home. But most of all, she kept urging her to eat that ebi.

As Jess talked, Frownie Face sometimes wagged her tail, sometimes whined a little, and, best of all, sometimes got up and crept just a little bit nearer to the ebi. Jess was afraid that an early-morning dog walker would come in and ruin everything, but the park remained empty and Frownie Face kept moving closer. She would have to pass Jess to get to the bowl, and when she did, Jess was ready. As the dog sidled by, Jess quickly clicked the leash onto her collar and then, just as quickly, moved the bowl right under her nose so Frownie Face couldn't help but lean down to gobble up the shrimp.

When Frownie Face was done eating, she started to move away, licking her lips, but Jess held tight. Frownie Face looked at her and barked, once. Jess was startled, but she kept talking and soothing and, after a while, Frownie Face stopped pulling and sat down beside her. Jess took out the brush, showed it to her and let her sniff it, then started brushing her. Frownie Face sighed and wagged and leaned against her legs, huffing up at her with ebi-smelling breath. Jess brushed and brushed, and then the two of them left the park together. On the way, Jess pulled down the paper so she could call Frownie Face's family and they could come and get their special lost dog, who wasn't lost anymore.

Later, Mugsy asked her wasn't she afraid that Frownie Face was going to bite her, but she never had been. Not even for one minute.

CHAPTER SIX:
FICTIVE KIN

"You're the anthropologist," said Ka-chan's new friend, Maureen. "What's it called when you're not really related but you're like family to each other anyway?"

"Fictive kin," said Ka-chan.

"Yeah, right, fictive kin." Maureen nodded. "That's what we're like, this potluck group. We've been getting together since the oldest kids were in kindergarten, so these guys have grown up with each other. It's been great! We're like this big group of lesbian aunties and gay uncles and the kids are like cousins."

Ka-chan and Mugsy shook their heads and laughed and said, "Wow, that's great!" and looked around at the room full of people. Jess's moms were happy as clams. Hank Clam and Cam Clam were happy, too. The house they were potlucking at had a playroom with even more Lego than the E-Ps had at home. All the littles were in there sitting around a huge pile that they had dumped out of a huge container.

"They're quiet now," Brad said. He was one of the dads whose house they were at.

"But after dessert, look out!" agreed Ben, the other dad. Those dads had a little girl named Kelly, the same age as Hank and Cam.

Ka-chan frowned at the mention of dessert. She didn't even know, thought Jess, who had already toured the kitchen with Aaron, a boy who was also going into second grade, and who she had met at church when she finally agreed to go to RE because the sermons were so boring. One entire kitchen counter was loaded with cookies and pie and some weird looking sticks that Aaron told her his moms had made and were pretzels dipped in chocolate and rainbow sprinkles.

Jess was taking her time with Aaron. She told Litka that he might be as good as their boys back home, but she wasn't sure. He was an only child, like Litka, and he told her he'd been adopted from a place called Guatemala. She'd been unlucky when she asked Mugsy about Guatemala, because her mom had been in full librarian mode and had talked at Jess forever, along with later bringing her a stack of books from the Robbins Library in downtown Arlington. Guatemala was a chunky, Lego-shaped country. Part of it abutted the Pacific Ocean and other parts abutted Belize, Mexico, Honduras and El Salvador. The kids in the books looked similar to Aaron, all right, with brown skin and straight black hair. Jess knew about adoption from one of the cohousing babies, but that baby had come from Springfield, which was still in Vermont. Aaron said he was only a baby when his moms got him from Guatemala, so he didn't remember anything about it. Arlington was all he knew, and he was an Arlingtonian.

"Mama Reese says I'm lucky to be here," Aaron said, when Jess mentioned that she liked Morrisville better than Arlington.

"Not me," said Jess. "It's bad luck for me to be here."

Everybody in Jess's family loved the fictive-kin potlucks. They had been to two so far, and Cam and Hank were already really good friends with Kelly and the other littles. Those boys were easy to please. Ka-chan and Mugsy were also all excited about the potlucks. They were always talking about the other moms and dads and going on and on about how great it was to have community here, how much they loved hanging out with other families like theirs, even though none of the other moms or dads were anything at all like the E-Ps.

The oldest fictive kin kids were in fifth grade already. Jess decided to like the potlucks because at the second one a fictive-kin fifth grader named Maeve got everyone playing stickball, and stickball was the best thing Jess had done in Arlington so far. It was a little bit like baseball, but you played with a plastic wiffle ball bat and a tennis ball. Everyone would go to the Brackett Elementary School basketball court and play stickball until all the moms and dads were ready to go home. Maeve was the queen of stickball.

Jess used allowance money to buy a wiffle ball set at the five-and-dime store, but she didn't need the ball itself, so she gave it to the twins, who took it down to the rumpus room where it disappeared into the sea of Lego. In the garage, Jess corked her new bat the way Maeve showed her.

First, you sliced off the top of the handle. Maeve said she might have to get a mom to do it for her, but Jess's knife worked perfectly for the job. Then you got pieces of newspaper, crumpled them up and used a stick to shove them all the way down into the bat and tamp them good. You didn't want to leave any air space. Then you sealed the bat back up and wrapped the handle with two different kinds of colored tape. The E-Ps only had duck tape from when everyone at cohousing had been making duck tape wallets, so Jess used that. Maeve said it would be ok, even though people usually used a different kind of tape.

Jess couldn't wait to try out her new bat and was really hoping Maeve would come to the next fictive kin potluck, which was going to be at the E-Ps' house, and she was also hoping that the good weather would hold. It had been so beautiful for so long that Jess was afraid it was a weather breeder. That's what it would mean in Vermont—bad weather always followed good weather—and people would have been getting ready for a storm. So far, in Arlington there had been some rainy days, but no storm.

Whenever there was a storm in Vermont, Oni would get really alert and pace through the house, trying to keep an eye on all the windows and doors. When the storm was over, he was always exhausted and would go to his bed in the kitchen and sleep for a really long time. If you tried to get him up to go outside or even to have his dinner, he would grumble at you, just opening one bleary eye, then curling back even tighter into an Oni ball, tuning everything out.

It had been eight weeks since they'd moved out of Holy Smoke. Jess was keeping track of the time on a calendar from a bank that had come in the mail. She liked this calendar because it had pictures of nature, like waterfalls and forests, and also, it had good advice about money. Now that she had earned $100 from capturing Frownie Face, she was more interested in bank stuff, especially since Mugsy had gone with her to open a savings account. They had put in the $100 as well as some birthday money that Obaa-san and Ojii-san had sent from Hawaii. Mugsy and Ka-chan had even added $10 of their own to sweeten the deal. If they were talking about the Deal where the E-Ps had to undergo great upheaval, Jess didn't think much could sweeten that, but if they were just talking about how it was a good deal that Jess had earned a Bill, then (fine.) That's what you called one hundred dollars: a Bill. Leonard had taught her that when he called to hear the outcome of Operation Capture Frownie Face.

"Eight years old, and the proud owner of a Bill," he'd said. "Right on!" Then Zack got on the phone and wanted to talk about the candy store again, but Jess had found that once she'd gotten the reward money and put it in the bank, she never felt like taking any of it out again. Even if it meant not having any candy worms.

The day of the fictive-kin potluck at the no-name house on Kenilworth St. in Arlington, on the first day of June, Jess's calendar gave the advice, "Stop putting off those home improvement projects! Consider refinancing your house for a low-interest home equity loan. Don't you think your family deserves to have a new roof before winter?" When Jess showed Mugsy, she said their roof was fine and, anyway, they were renting and the roof here wasn't their responsibility.

"What about Holy Smoke?" asked Jess.

"Holy Smoke is solid as a brick," said Mugsy. "Stop with the corporate advice already!" Then she shooed her away and called out to Ka-chan, who was trying to get Hank and Cam to help clean up the rumpus room, "Do you think Ben is coming? Did he say? Because if so, I'm going to hide those bottles of dandelion wine Lulu sent us!" Ka-chan hollered up, "Ooh, you're so bad!" and both her moms laughed and Mugsy shooed her again before she could ask what was so darn funny.

It turned out that the nice days weren't a weather breeder, or at least not yet, because the potluck day was just as nice, if not nicer, than the whole week had been. Stickball was a bust, though, because Maeve and her moms weren't coming. Ka-chan said they were in Ireland visiting Maeve's Irish grandparents. Jess already knew that Ireland was an island near England because she'd gone through the whole ask-Mugsy-get-too-much-information thing after she'd read a book called *Irish Tales and Sagas* back when she was in her tales phase: tall, fairy and otherwise. These days, she preferred stories about real people, even though she still found herself drifting nearer and nearer whenever Ka-chan read to the twins from their current favorite, *Native American Animal Stories*.

"Why don't *you* get a stickball game going?" asked Mugsy, which showed how much she knew. Jess shrugged and firmly put her bat away in the garage. If you started to explain to Mugsy that Maeve was the only one who could do stickball and that the fifth graders wouldn't take any suggestions from her, a new kid and only an almost-second-grader, Mugsy would just argue. She would probably use some homeschooling arguments, too, like it's ability and interest that matter, not age, look how you and Leonard get along because you're both interested in tai chi, or how you taught New York City Pete from cohousing how to tell a sugar maple from a pine tree.

Just thinking about how Mugsy might argue about stickball made Jess mad. Mugsy didn't get to use those homeschooling arguments if she was going to send her only daughter to horrible, miserable Brackett Elementary School. Case closed.

It turned out that only two fifth graders came, anyway, Joelle and Lilly, and they drifted off together after the meal. Jess heard them tell Lilly's dad that they were going over to the park and, after they left, he told the rest of the grownups that they were probably going to go sit in the playhouse at the park and gossip, because just this summer they'd "discovered boys" and everyone laughed. Hank and Cam and Katie and two other littles were in the rumpus room swimming around in the Lego sea, so that left Jess in charge of the rest of the kids, who were all first and second graders: Aaron, second grade; Arlington-Zack, second grade; and Marie-Louise, first grade, whose family was from France and who spoke a very interesting kind of English. Her nickname was "Malou."

Jess had been prepared to like Arlington-Zack because he had such a good name, and also Ka-chan and his mom, Maureen, were super best friends now. She didn't know him too well, yet. When the potluck had been at his house last time, he'd begged and begged Maureen to let the kids get on the Wii, and even though she said no at first, she finally got ground down. Luckily, Jess knew how to play "that thing," as Mugsy called it, because Dre's grandparents had one at their house.

"Do you have a computer in your room? Or anything else fun?" Arlington-Zack asked now. "Let's go up there and see!"

Jess didn't know what he meant by fun, but she didn't have any technology in her room. The E-P moms didn't believe in it. Except Ka-chan had to buy a laptop for grad school, but that was her private property. And they did have a computer, right in the living room. But, other than that, no Wii or anything.

"Do you have a kitty or a doggie?" Malou wanted to know. She said "keetie" and "dehggie" which made Arlington-Zack laugh in a little bit of a mean way.

"I have a dog back home in Vermont," said Jess. "He can't live here because he doesn't know how to walk on a leash. And I think we're going to get a cat if my brothers can convince my moms."

"She captured a runaway dog, though!" said Aaron, who loved hearing the story about the ebi and the Escapee. That was something Jess had in her room, she thought, the newspaper story about how she returned Frownie Face to her family when even the animal officer had failed. A reporter and a photographer had interviewed her and taken her picture with the Chalmers family, who were the people Frownie Face had escaped from. They lived

73

on a street called George over near another elementary school, but it turned out their kids were grown up, so the story Jess had told Frownie Face about the kids crying because they missed her had been a lie by accident.

Upstairs, Aaron and Malou sat on Jess's floor and waited for her to tell them what was next, but Arlington-Zack roamed around, opening drawers and looking out the window. Jess wondered what he was looking for. She got out the newspaper article that she had pasted into her memory book. There were a lot of pictures of Oni in there, too, some taken with a camera, and some that were drawn. One of her favorites was a sketch that Lulu had made of Oni, Nip and Tuck herding sheep. It was just a few lines drawn with charcoal, but it had so much energy, she and Mugsy agreed, that the dogs looked like they could leap off the page.

Arlington-Zack looked at the book with the others for just a few moments, and interrupted her story about capturing Frownie Face. "A hundred dollars isn't that much. Where's your tv?"

"We don't have one," said Jess. "My moms don't like tv." Deal with it, she said in her head, looking right at him. That's what Ka-chan always said when the answer came back no, again, every time she and her brothers asked the moms for the millionth time if they could get a tv.

74

"That's stupid," Arlington-Zack said. "Everyone has a tv!"

"My *mémère* doesn't!" said Malou. Jess wondered if that was French for Grandma, but she didn't get a chance to ask.

"Where's the bathroom?" asked Arlington-Zack.

Jess went down the hall to show him, and had just started setting up her Vermont monopoly game with the others when Arlington-Zack came stomping back into the room.

"You know what's gross?" he said loudly, and everyone looked up at him. "There was pee in the toilet!"

"So what?" asked Jess. "If it's yellow, let it mellow. If it's brown, flush it down!" That's what Ka-chan had taught them, and she had learned it from a friend of hers in college, who maybe was her girlfriend before she met Mugsy, and who was from California where there was a water shortage. "It saves water if you don't flush every time."

"It's disgusting," said Arlington-Zack. He had a sick look on his face. "It's dirty. I'm going downstairs."

Jess got a strange, squinched feeling in her stomach from what Arlington-Zack had said. She looked around her room, which was filled with twigs and feathers and bird nests. She wondered if

75

he thought it was dirty. It was certainly nature-y. And he maybe thought it was dirty and weird that she had some of Oni's hair in a ball on the windowsill next to her bed. And that there was a mason jar full of pond water on her desk that was a microcosm she had made in RE back home—but it maybe hadn't liked the ride down to Arlington, because the water had started to cloud up and look a little slimy. She also thought about the bathroom, about going into someone's bathroom and finding someone else's pee in the toilet, the pee of someone you didn't even know.

Jess and Aaron and Malou played Vermont Monopoly for a long time and it was really fun because it turned out that Malou was a Monopoly fiend, even though this was the first time she'd ever played and Jess and Aaron had to explain everything to her. But the whole time, in the back of her mind, Jess was thinking about Arlington-Zack, who never came back upstairs. Thinking about how he didn't like her room with no technology and how he thought her bathroom was gross. Maybe she didn't really like Arlington-Zack, but even more than that, she thought he must not like her. He didn't like her, he didn't like her house and he didn't like how her moms ran things. It was a queasy, uneasy feeling not to be liked.

Malou got up and pumped her fist in the air

just then. She'd been scheming and dealing and wheeling and had finally managed to buy the most expensive property in the game, Church Street. Jess laughed as Aaron rolled around going, "No way, no way! She's going to win!" but that uneasy feeling remained. Jess guessed there wasn't going to be any getting around Arlington-Zack being her fictive kin, but that didn't mean she had to sister him up. She would just have to stay out of his way. And hope like crazy that he wouldn't be in her class at horrible, miserable Brackett Elementary School.

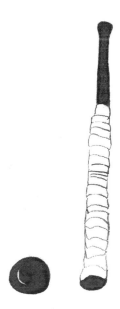

CHAPTER SEVEN:
A POOL IN THE NEIGHBORHOOD

It was pretty hot in Arlington in the summer. Jess wished she could go swimming somewhere on her own, like she could at the swimming hole back home. At the Arlington swimming hole, which was called the Res, you needed a grownup to take you. Across the street from their new house, two little girls had a baby pool in the front yard, and when they played in it their beagle barked at them from the porch where he was tied up. When it was really hot, Jess wished she could join them.

One Saturday in June, Jess had to put on her tie-dye t-shirt and brush her hair because they were going into Boston with some of the fictive kin to a big parade called Pride. Even though she didn't like crowds, Jess was curious about Pride because Mugsy and Ka-chan were Over the Moon about this opportunity for the kids to see Community and had been talking about it all week. "More gay people in one place than you've ever seen in your life!" Mugsy said happily. "I'm just Over the Moon about it!" "Waaay Over the Moon!" Ka-chan agreed. The moms were getting dressed up, too, and Ben and Brad had given the twins matching t-shirts that said, "I Love My Two Moms"—and Mugsy didn't say a peep, even though she hated dressing the twins alike. Katie had one that said, "I Love My Two Dads," and the three littles were already marching around like nobody's business in the front yard as they waited for everyone to gather so they could go to the Alewife T station together.

Jess had gotten the same t-shirt as the twins, but Mugsy said she didn't have to wear it, which was a relief. It was itchy and the sleeves and neck were weird, and plus, she didn't like t-shirts that said things, except for a very special one Leonard had given her when they left home that said, "Vermont is Full of Loons" with a beautiful picture of a loon on it. He also had given her a post card of the state of Vermont, which is shaped like a Lego piece, and written on it, "Vermont will have one less loon until you come home again!" She had that taped to the wall of her room.

Sitting on the driveway wall thinking about loons and a little bit about Lego, Jess saw Mikey-from-two-houses-down come out, walking fast. They knew each other from when his puppy had almost peed on her foot, and then it turned out he lived right on their street. Mikey passed in front of the house, but he was in such a hurry that he didn't notice her. Or maybe he did; sometimes people here didn't say hi. He was wearing a swimsuit and carrying a towel, and it wasn't the first time Jess had seen him dressed like that and going somewhere. Did he have a friend who had a pool? Just then, everyone started rushing around, telling her to get in the car, so she didn't see where he was going. If he was going to a house that had a pool, it couldn't be anywhere on her street, because she knew everyone's backyards inside and out by now. She'd just have to keep her eye on him.

Riding in the subway—the T—was loud and friendly and full of rainbows. There were already more gay people on the train than Jess had seen in her whole life, and they were all in a really good mood. A very tall lady with a beard bent down and slipped rainbow bead necklaces over all the kids' heads, saying, "Happy Pride, next generation!" and Ben said, "It's already a perfect Pride—we've been blessed by a Radical Faerie!"

"What's that?" asked Hank, and Mugsy got an explain-y look on her face, but just then someone with a ukulele started singing "Somewhere Over the Rainbow" and everyone joined in. Mugsy wouldn't forget, though, and Jess was sure there would be a big lesson about those faeries somewhere in the future.

There were even more gay people when they got off the train at a station called Park Street. The fictive kin found a place to watch the parade by a fence in the shade and set up a whole camp, with a blanket to sit on and a cooler full of drinks and snacks. Ben and Maureen went off to get donuts, which Ka-chan let them have, even though she really, really didn't approve of sugary things for breakfast. But the (fictive) kin always had donuts on Pride, and anthropologists have to go along with the people they're with so they can study the culture. Ka-chan was full of anthropological knowledge now that she'd started summer classes at grad school.

Mugsy said, "What the heck, woman, can't we just enjoy some donuts if they come our way?" and Ka-chan looked surprised, and then she laughed and gave Mugsy a hug. Her moms were happy with all the other happy people, and it made them so silly. Everyone was eating donuts and talking fast and laughing a ton. Jess pretended she had to be in charge of Hank and Cam and Katie so she wouldn't have to hang out with Arlington-Zack, who had a Game Boy and wasn't paying very much attention anyway. Ever since he'd found pee in the upstairs toilet at her house, Arlington-Zack didn't have a lot to say to Jess. Maeve and the other fifth graders were there, though, and they were friendly.

"Just get ready," Maeve told her. "There's candy and necklaces."

Some of the fictive kin were marching in the parade, like Malou and Aaron and their moms. "Maybe next year, we can march, too," said Mugsy. "Wouldn't that be fun?"

Definitely, gay or not, Jess had never seen so many people in one place before in her life. She felt a little nervous, but she copied the fifth graders, who were getting set up right on the curb. After the leather-wearing motorcycle ladies went by, she understood why, because almost everyone marching or riding slowly by on floats would throw something, and they liked to throw to kids. There were more of the rainbow bead necklaces, some of them with blinky lights, and candy and t-shirts and pencils and pens and things in little crinkly packages that Ka-chan took, saying, "I'll just keep this for now," in her voice that meant it was a grownup thing.

One float that the entire E-P family liked the best was the one that looked like a sailing ship with everyone on it dressed up as pirates and singing a song that had "Yo ho ho!" in it. "Gay pirates!" Mugsy kept saying. "Who knew?" What Jess knew—and pretty quickly, too—is stay away from Arlington-Zack during the Pride parade, because he snatched things that were obviously meant for you.

The next day, the E-Ps went to church and the moms even went up and lit a candle and said how glad they were for the Pride parade and for Community. In RE, Jess had to be partners with Arlington-Zack because Aaron wasn't there, and that put her in a bad mood.

"Stop hanging around," said Mugsy when they got home. She was in the kitchen, humming as she started making Sunday dinner. "If you don't want to go to the park with Ka-chan and the boys, why don't you go do some weeding? That always makes you feel better."

A while back, Jess and Mugsy had gone to a nursery for plants and gotten some impatiens and johnny jump ups and other flowers to put in front of the house. Jess went out and started tending to them, because Mugsy was right: doing stuff with dirt and plants did make her feel better. The cat from next door, William, came and sat with her. William liked everybody, even dogs, but he hated other cats. That's what his person had told her one time.

William was a large, orange, puffy guy with a round belly and extra toes. "Polydactyl," Mugsy said. "'Poly' meaning more than one, 'dactyl' meaning digits, or toes."

"Hello, Mr. Polydactyl," said Jess. Cats made her feel better, too. Best of all would be Oni, of course. William butted her with his big head and purred. His tail looked like a feather boa.

A door slammed and Jess didn't even look up. Somewhere in the back of her mind she had been waiting for Mikey to come out of his house, and she was sure that this was him. Yup, she could see him out of the corner of her eye, hurrying down the street carrying his towel. He went right past her, but this time it wasn't weird that he didn't say anything, because she was hunched down behind some bushes and he probably didn't see her. As soon as he was past, she scooched over to the sidewalk and slowly stood up, casually dusting off her hands and brushing off her knees and the seat of her pants.

With William following her, his tail sticking straight up in the air, Jess strolled down the walk, going in the direction Mikey had gone but pretending she was going around the block for reasons of her own. She kept Mikey in view. He turned down Hawthorne and then started running, his towel flapping. Jess walked faster, leaving William behind, but didn't run herself, as that would look suspicious. Mikey turned on Oakland and screeched into a driveway halfway down the street.

Jess walked by fast, like she was going somewhere important. She could see down the driveway and sure enough, there was an inground pool. Mikey was sitting on the edge and there were some other kids there, too, but she didn't recognize anyone. No fictive kin. She slowed down for another quick look, and just as she walked by the garage, a boy came out carrying a bag of potato chips. He sat down on the steps and looked at her. She stopped and looked back. She'd never seen him before.

"You like barbeque flavor?" he asked, opening the bag and holding it out to her.

"Sure." Jess moved closer and took a few chips. He took some, too.

"Is that your pool?" Jess asked.

"Yep. But we can't eat near it. We have ants."

Jess stood in front of him for a while then sat down on the steps. They ate the whole bag of chips. When it was empty, the boy went back around to his pool and she continued on down the street, listening to the whooping and splashing.

From then on, Jess couldn't stop thinking about the boy with the pool. She thought about all the different ways he might invite her to go swimming. Maybe he would tell Mikey that he could invite her. She made sure to be in the front yard a lot, and she did see Mikey on his way to the pool a couple more times that week, but he never said anything to her; well, once he said, "Hi." Another way she might get to swim in the pool was if she saw the boy sitting on the steps again and he asked her if she liked to swim and she would say, "Sure," in a relaxed way and then he might ask her to come on by later in the afternoon, or even say that he would wait while she went and got her suit and then he would show her the pool. He might ask her if she could dive, which she could.

One other way might be if there was a pool party and the parents of the boy might say, "Wouldn't it be nice to invite all the kids in the neighborhood? Didn't a new girl move in to that blue house on Kenilworth? Why don't you go ask her?"

The next time she was at the grocery store with Mugsy, Jess even begged her to get barbeque potato chips, even though potato chips were not on the approved shopping list for the E-Ps. Mugsy just looked at her like she was an alien dropped down from Planet Who-Knows-Where and kept loading up the shopping cart with things like broccoli.

Every morning in Arlington, Jess kept to her 5 a.m. wake-up schedule. She liked how secret things could happen before the sun was fully up, even here in Arlington. So far on her early morning expeditions, Jess had seen two raccoons run across the road in front of her and skitter up a tree. When she stood quietly for a long time under the tree, one of them had started to come back down but had made a terrible squeak when it saw her and skittered back, even further up in the branches.

On the way to the park in the early morning, she had also seen the very sad sight of a run-over possum, it's long skinny tail smashed and its small, toothy muzzle slightly open. Later when she went back to look more closely, the possum was gone, and Mugsy told her probably the animal officer had come to pick it up. That's what happened to the run-over squirrels they saw, as well.

"How would you like to have that job, eh?" asked Mugsy, but then she didn't wait for Jess's answer, which was that she would consider it, especially since she for sure knew she could handle catching animal escapees.

Every morning, Ka-chan left four quarters on the kitchen counter by the back door so Jess could go up to the bus stop on Park Ave. by the water tower to buy a paper. There were two machines for selling papers, and Jess thought the *Boston Herald* looked more interesting, because it always had funny headlines in big letters like "YA GOTTA BE KIDDING, MR. PATRICK!!" But Ka-chan said to get the other one, the *Boston Globe.* "If I wanted to read schlock, I would read the *National Enquirer*," she said, and Mugsy said, "Or *Oprah*," which was a magazine Ka-chan did read and said it was schlock, but important schlock, and the conversation might go on from there until Ka-chan said loudly, "One woman's schlock is another woman's treasure!"

On her way to get the paper one morning, Jess passed a house where all the windows were open and she could smell coffee and toast smells coming out. Just as she passed the kitchen window, someone inside burped. It wasn't the loudest burp Jess had ever heard, but it startled her and she jumped. Then the person inside burped again, and this time, it *was* the loudest burp she'd ever heard. It sounded like a motorcycle, the way it started kind of soft and grumbly, then grew and grew and grew:

bbbbBBBBBBrrrrRRRRRRaaaaAAAAAPPPP!!!

It was a mighty, mighty burp, and it stopped Jess in her tracks. She gasped, then let out a yelp of laughter. After a moment, the person inside started to laugh, too. For a moment, they were laughing together, but then Jess heard the person start walking and she was afraid they would come look out the window at her, so she got going, running so fast she almost dropped her quarters.

Later, after everyone had had breakfast and Ka-chan had read the paper and gone off to summer grad school, Mugsy asked them what they wanted to do in the remaining weeks of summer before their own schools got going. She had explained that there were two more weeks before the boys started preschool and then one more after that before she started her job at the Robbins Library and Jess would be staying with Maureen and Arlington-Zack during the day until horrible, miserable Brackett started. Mugsy didn't say the "horrible, miserable" part. Both her moms loved their new friend Maureen, Arlington-Zack's mom. They knew Jess didn't care for Arlington-Zack very much, but they thought it was because the two kids didn't know each other very well yet.

"You have no problem getting along with boys," Mugsy said when Jess told her she'd prefer not to spend time with Arlington-Zack. "Not this boy," muttered Jess, but she could tell the wheels of adult business were grinding over her preferences. Maybe they would relent and let her go visit the boys (and girl) she did get along with in Vermont, but they said they weren't ready to let her go on the bus all by herself and nobody could come get her and they couldn't leave to take her. It would be no problem to go on the bus, Jess argued, but they kept saying no.

"A boy in this neighborhood has a swimming pool in his backyard," blurted out Jess, after the twins had suggested a lot of different activities for the rest of the summer, like marrying President Obama, recycling strawberry ice cream and something in Twin Language that sounded like "skipsnipillipple".

"Really?" Mugsy looked sharply at Jess. "Should we go to the Res today?" Jess shook her head, even though she liked that the town swimming hole was next to a tiny farm—a real one growing food, not just a park—and there were interesting stickery, floaty black seeds you could collect, but you had to be careful not to step on them because they could really poke a hole in a person. "A pool in the neighborhood, eh?" said Mugsy. "Ok. I'm on it."

It was just that Jess wanted to swim in that pool so badly. She hoped that asking Mugsy for help was a shortcut to what probably was going to happen naturally any day: that is, she would get invited by the boy or by the boy's friends. She also really hoped the other kids wouldn't know that her mom had helped with this. Because Mugsy worked fast; Jess could hardly bear to watch.

First, Mugsy got on the phone and called

Maureen, who had actually been born in Arlington and had never left, and Maureen told her the name of the boy's family and a history of their whole lives that Mugsy thought was interesting but Jess thought was a waste of time, because why didn't Mugsy just hang up and get on with it already?

Jess left to go weed the flowers, and when she came back, Mugsy was still on the phone, going, "No kidding! You have got to be kidding me!" Jess went back outside. Now would be a good time for Mikey to come out with his towel and say, "Hey, come on! Everyone's invited today!" and the waiting would be over, but he didn't. Instead, William came around and rubbed up against her. He was a very silky fellow. Jess liked how his mouth opened a little when he was purring, and if you got close enough, you could smell his kitty breath and get tickled by his whiskers. His fur smelled good, too.

"Woo-hoo!" she heard Mugsy shout. "Jess! Come here! You will be amazed! I am soooo good!" When Jess got into the living room, Mugsy was doing a victory dance in a circle, holding hands with Hank and Cam, who were totally cracking up. "I am a mistress at pulling the neighborhood strings!" said Mugsy. "I am a suburban Wonder Woman, navigating the currents of middle-class rivers to finesse an invitation for my rural Wonder Children to the fabled inground pool in the backyard of the doughty O'Connells!" All of which complicated talk meant that the whole family was invited to the pool tomorrow. Mugsy bumped fists with the twins and tried to bump with Jess, but Jess stepped aside.

"Are other kids going to be there, or just us?"

"I think you mean, 'Thank you, Mugsy, oh goddess among women, for figuring out how to get an invite to the pool party!'" said Mugsy.

"ThankyouMugsyohgoddessamongwomen," mumbled Jess. Mugsy was always making them say that. She repeated, "Are other kids going to be there?"

"You're thinking that, well, you'll get to swim in the pool, but the social introduction that you're looking for with the neighborhood posse will continue to be out of your reach?" asked Mugsy. She was really proud of herself. "Your mother Mugsy," Ka-chan might say if she were here, "has a very high opinion of herself."

"I guess," said Jess. "So will there?"

"Well, having anticipated this very situation, I asked that same question, my darling daughter, and Oscar's parental unit—did I tell you the young person in question has the old-fashioned name of Oscar?—the parental unit answered ...," she paused, smiling and nodding. The twins were laughing and getting excited about the pool. They didn't care who else was there since everyone else was just gravy to their twin world.

"What?" Jess practically screamed. Had it really been worth it to enlist Mugsy? That was actually the question.

"He answered: Yes! Yes! There will be many other kids! Because tomorrow is the traditional yearly Open Pool event and he was deeply apologetic that he had neglected to invite us but he had not been informed that there was a family with kids newly moved onto Kenilworth, as he is a busy executive who cannot know what all is going on just mere streets from his own abode."

"What?"

Mugsy got herself a drink of water and finally calmed down. She started throwing some snacks into a bag. "Jess, sweetie, there's going to be an Open Pool Party tomorrow for everyone in the neighborhood, and we're all going to go. It's really good you asked me to call, because otherwise we might not have known about it. So we're going, and there are going to be all the kids in the neighborhood. Happy, honey?"

You had to say yes, but why was everything so complicated with grownups? Why couldn't Jess get on a bus and go visit her friends in Vermont? Why had Mugsy started worrying about Jess going out early in the morning by herself to "roam through the neighborhood"? Why did Arlington have to be the worst place on earth?

Jess retired to her room to try and get in a better mood. She read her Vermont wildlife magazine until Mugsy yelled up that they were going out to Concord to get a handle on that ol' Revolutionary War and all the kids had better hop like bunnies into the car. Jess closed her magazine and looked in the mirror. Ka-chan would tell her to brush her hair but Mugsy wouldn't. She could hear Mugsy and the twins singing, "Sooooome bunny loves you!" downstairs and just then, just like that, she got an excited, tingly feeling in her stomach. She was going to a pool party!

earlier,
half-page

CHAPTER EIGHT:
POCKETKNIFE

Even after she'd had a bath, Jess could smell chlorine on her skin. She stood stock still in the living room and took a sniff of her wrist. Chlorine. From Oscar's pool. All the rest of that month, after that first time at the pool party, she had spent most afternoons swimming. She wouldn't tell anyone, seeing as how she was known as a nature girl, but she secretly truly loved the inground cement pool, even more than where they used to swim in Vermont.

The water in the inground pool was clear to the bottom. When spiders and moths got caught in the water, you could rescue them with a net on the end of a long pole. One end of the pool was deep enough for diving, which you could do without worrying about hitting a hidden rock or snag, and the other end was shallow enough that you could just hang out there, talking and staying cool, and fish wouldn't nibble at your ankles because there weren't any. Cannonballs were always a great idea. It was cannonballing that made Oscar and Mikey like her, Jess knew.

She was really, really good at cannonballs. They thought she would be afraid that first time, and probably she should have waited so as not to splash all the parents who were lying out in the sun, but she just went ahead and bombed it and after that it was ok with them for her to throw on her suit, grab her towel and head on over. Any time after 1 p.m. was the rule, but if the gate was locked, it meant that Oscar's mom had to run an errand so there wouldn't be a grownup around and you couldn't swim. That was always a bummer, when that happened.

Oscar and Mikey were both going into third grade, and at first they treated her like a little kid, but that didn't last long. She wished they were going to be in the same class, but they weren't even going to be in the same school, because they both went to St. Agnes, which was a private school for Catholics. Catholics were a kind of church-goer, but not the same as UUs, which is what the E-Ps were. "And unfortunately, they don't always like our kind," said Ka-chan.

When Mugsy and Ka-chan said "our kind" they meant being gay. Luckily, none of this ever came up when Jess was over at Oscar's, and Mugsy told Ka-chan that Oscar's family seemed to be "love the sinner, hate the sin" kind of people and then started to explain to Jess that that meant they might not approve of gayness, but they were going to be nice to gay people anyway, and she was about to say a lot more on the subject when Jess held up her palm and said, "Mugsy, talk to the hand!" That was something useful she'd learned over at Oscar's, but it ended up getting her sent to her room for a time-out.

The pool had saved Jess from her days with Arlington-Zack. Sure enough, just like they had talked about at family meeting, Mugsy had started her job at Robbins Library, Cam and Hank did preschool and Jess was supposed to go to Arlington-Zack's house. The first day, Maureen tried to get the two of them to hang out together and Jess did try to play the PS2, but Arlington-Zack obviously didn't want to and just made a lot of comments about how she wasn't very good at this game and didn't they have PS2 in Vermont? Lunch at Arlington-Zack's was unappetizing. It was something called Lunch Pacs where everything came wrapped in plastic on a plastic tray. Cheese, crackers, dried-up celery sticks with sweet-tasting peanut butter and a cookie. Arlington-Zack said Lunch Pacs were his favorite, but he mostly just ate the crackers and the cookie.

"Now you two can run along to the pool," said Maureen, who had some work she wanted to do on the computer, but Arlington-Zack said no way was he going to that loser's pool, so Jess went by herself. No problem. Mugsy picked her up after work, and that's how it went most days, except she started bringing her book and reading while Arlington-Zack did the PS2.

Jess smelled her wrist again and then tasted it. Mmm, chlorine! Today had been the last pool day. Even though the weather was still hot enough to swim, Oscar said his parents were very strict about closing the pool once school started. Nobody but them thought it was a good rule, but no one could convince them to change their minds. Mugsy said, "Give the poor woman a break! She's been watching over you kids all summer, making sure you don't drown. She needs a rest!" Nobody had ever been close to drowning, Jess told her, and Oscar's mom always seemed relaxed and happy to have kids over, and Mugsy said, "Fine, ok, but still."

Tomorrow was the first day of school. The name of Jess's second-grade teacher was Mrs. Bilder. Jess had met her and the principal, Mrs.

Epsilon, last week, just because not too many people came into the school from being homeschooled and the grownups wanted Jess to see what she was getting into. Not that she had a choice.

"I would prefer to homeschool," Jess said to her moms, and they just nodded and looked at her sadly. They'd already had this conversation a few million times. School it was, and school it was going to be.

"It's school, ok," said Hank to her after one of the millions of conversations. "We preschool no problem-o." He put his sticky hand on her arm and then kissed her on the inside of the elbow. Cam kissed her other elbow.

"Thanks," said Jess. "You guys really like preschool?"

Cam took some Lego pieces out of his pocket and started lining them up on the floor next to her. Hank ran off and came back with a Tupperware of all red pieces and dumped them out. Jess had to scrunch up to avoid the tide of Lego.

"Play!" Cam ordered, so Jess gave up being mad about school, and by suppertime the three of them had over twenty fabulous Lego creatures and Ka-chan took a picture.

Mrs. Bilder was a white lady about as old as the Old Guy, with bright orange hair the color of clown hair. When Mugsy told Teresa, Jess's tutor, the name of Jess's teacher, Teresa said, "Oh, mmm-hmm," and Mugsy said, "What?" and Teresa said, "Oh, I'm sure it will be fine. Mrs. Bilder is just, shall we say, looking forward to retiring."

"Do you think she'll have a problem with the two-mom thing?" asked Mugsy, and Teresa shook her head. "She's been around the block a few hundred times," she said, and when Jess asked, Teresa told her that meant Mrs. Bilder had a lot of experience so that nothing surprised her anymore. Which did not end up being true.

The whole family took Jess to school the first day. She was wearing some new jeans shorts with good pockets they had found at a thrift store in a place called Davis Square, where there was also a Japanese restaurant that Ka-chan approved of. Jess was wearing her Vermont loon shirt, and Ka-chan had brushed her hair and slicked down the cowlicks with something clear blue and smelly out of a tube.

"Our daughter with greasy kid stuff in her hair!" said Mugsy.

On the way over to school, Jess saw some of the boys and girls she'd been swimming with for the past few weeks, looking different with school clothes on. More grown up, which made it a little hard to know what to say to them. Ahead of them,

Jess saw a boy and a woman holding hands. As soon as they stepped into the park, the boy dropped the woman's hand and stepped away from her. The woman bent down to kiss his head, and he jerked away and the woman laughed.

"Oh, it's Maureen and Zack!" said Mugsy. "Hey, you guys!"

Arlington-Zack's shoulders stiffened with embarrassment because he knew Jess had seen him holding his mother's hand. He tugged at his new Yu-Gi-Oh shirt and said something to her in a low voice, which she couldn't quite hear but could tell was mean. Jess was so nervous she barely paid any attention. Before they left the house, the E-Ps had done a family hug and walked along holding hands for a block before the twins broke away and started running. Mugsy and Ka-chan were still holding hands. In the books about Ramona Quimby and Henry Huggins, Henry's dog Ribsy always went to school with the kids and then waited for Henry to get out in the afternoon. For a minute, Jess was almost angry at Oni for not knowing how to be a dog in the suburbs. If he could be waiting for her later, that would help her so much with this school situation.

"You have a mat," Hank explained to her. "And a cubby."

"Snack!" chimed in Cam.

"I know," said Jess. "I'll be ok, guys. See you later!"

Someone showed her where to line up on the playground. She saw Aaron in another line, behind a man teacher, and they waved. Then a bell rang and she was walking inside.

"Good morning, boys and girls," said Mrs. Bilder. She was standing in front of the class with a big fake-y smile on her face. "Welcome to your first day of second grade! We have a lot of work to do this year, so I'm going to expect you to act like big kids. No goofing off! Do you understand me? If you understand me, say, 'Yes, Mrs. Bilder!'"

Jess joined in as everyone said, "Yes, Mrs. Bilder," then Mrs. Bilder made them say it again because she said she couldn't hear them the first time. Jess had been relieved to be assigned a seat next to Sarah, a girl who came to Oscar's pool sometimes and was funny and nice, even though she never did any cannonballs. Sarah had been glad to see her, too, and didn't pretend not to know her, like Arlington-Zack was doing. Mugsy had already told her, but until she saw him in line on the playground behind Mrs. Bilder, Jess had really hoped there'd been a mistake, but no, they really were in the same class, and she was going to have to see him every day along with Oliver, Reese, Shane, Ben, Jake, Liam, Kevin, Claudia, Elise,

Elyse, Grace, Julia, Maya, Lisa, Lucy, Nick, Austin, Lindsey, Greta, Kathleen, Cate and Sarah. Everybody but Arlington-Zack seemed really nice and some of them were even smiling at her across the room. Mrs. Bilder was still talking about homework, but Jess was too nervous to pay attention. She put her hand in her pocket and snuck a touch of her pocketknife.

The familiar curves were soothing. She held the whole thing in her hand for a moment, feeling its good weight. Mrs. Bilder looked over at her sharply, and Jess quickly pulled her hand out of her pocket. Both Mugsy and Ka-chan had told her that she was absolutely, positively not to take her pocketknife to school. They made her promise she would leave her knife at home, safe in her dresser drawer. They said there were very strict rules about knives and school. But there was no way the teacher could know what was in her pocket. She didn't have x-ray vision or anything.

Jess put both hands on her desk and tried to listen. Mrs. Bilder gave her one more look, then turned around and wrote something on the board. "Class, this is your homework for tomorrow," she said, and everyone groaned. "That's right, young people!" said Mrs. Bilder, with another big, fake-y smile. "Homework on the first day of school! You're second graders, now!"

Jess made it through the morning without touching her knife again, but by recess, she was burning with the desire to whittle something. As the kids spilled outside, she looked all around for a quiet corner where she could be by herself. She saw some of the fictive-kin fifth graders playing basketball with a tall, lanky fifth-grade teacher. Maeve gave her a friendly salute and called out, "Stickball later?"

"You know her?" asked Sarah, impressed, and Jess nodded but didn't go into the whole fictive-kin thing. It had never come up at the pool, but what if Sarah was Catholic? Best not to take any chances by giving out too much information. "Come on!" shouted Sarah, and for a little while Jess forgot about her knife as Sarah and a bunch of other girls taught her how to play Night at the Museum.

After recess, for all the time before lunch, Mrs. Bilder made them do spelling worksheets. The worksheets weren't hard, but they were boring, and Mrs. Bilder came around looking at everyone's writing. "Make this straighter," she told Jess, tapping on Jess's letter A, so Jess drew it again and Mrs. Bilder nodded. "Quite different from being homeschooled, I imagine!" she said, and everyone looked up at Jess and one boy asked, "What's that?" but Mrs. Bilder shushed him. Jess's face felt hot as she leaned over her desk. She wanted to touch her knife.

Lunch was kind of fun. Mugsy had given Jess some money for the first day, saying, "You see what the school food is like, and if you want, we can sign you up for a lunch plan, or we can send you with homemade lunch. You be the decider." Sarah showed Jess how to get a tray and go through the lunch line. There was a hamburger and french fries and some broccoli that looked a little gray. Most people weren't eating the broccoli, but Jess gave it a try. Salty and mushy, but doable. The hamburger was good, too, and Jess loved french fries, so maybe buying lunch was what she would decide to do. The tables in the cafeteria were round with attached stools shooting off them like petals on a flower. It was so crowded that Jess and Sarah had to share a stool, so each of them just had one part of their butt on and it was a little tippy, but no problem really.

After lunch, they had recess again, and Sarah and Jess got to the tetherball first, so they played that the whole time. Jess liked punching the ball and seeing it go winding around the pole on its string, and even though she'd never played before, Sarah said she was really good. Jess was glad to feel the weight of her knife in her pocket as she played but didn't really think about whittling until she was back in class. Then she could hardly wait to get out of there so she could go home. She had a stash of good whittling sticks in her closet and had gotten a lot better at it since that first time when she'd nicked her finger. But after school, Maeve saw her and told her to run home and get her bat because they were having a stickball tournament, and it lasted a pretty long time, especially since they had to have a discussion if this one boy, Eric, would be allowed to play since he'd cheated last time by corking his bat with pennies so it would be heavier and could hit the ball farther. Some kids wanted to ban him, but Maeve said, "Nah, he won't do it again," and even picked him for her team.

After that, it was supper time, and then they had a family meeting to check in about Jess's first day of school and then Ka-chan made her do her homework, which took almost until dark. By that time, Jess was so tired, all she could do was sit and listen to the Mrs. Pepperpot book Mugsy was reading to the twins. She ended up falling asleep in Cam's bed and Mugsy had to carry her back to her own room, and she never did brush her teeth.

Jess took her knife to school with her every day all that first week, and then the next week, too. Throughout the school day, the urge to whittle would come and go. It was especially strong when Mrs. Bilder was in front of the class talking about spelling. Jess had stopped putting her hand in her pocket to touch her knife, because she could tell that Mrs. Bilder didn't like it, but she would shift in her seat so she could feel the comforting weight against her thigh. She'd figured out that there weren't any safe places to whittle outside on the playground and, anyway, recess was the best time of school. The only place she let herself take out her knife was in the bathroom, when she could shut herself in a stall. Usually once a day, and sometimes more, she would get the bathroom pass and take out her knife in private, opening the blades, testing their sharpness and polishing them on her jeans.

Mrs. Bilder was punishing Arlington-Zack for scribbling on his desk. He was standing in front of the room and she was telling the class what he had done and why it was bad. Arlington-Zack was blushing and looking like he was going to cry. Jess raised her hand and asked for the bathroom pass, and Mrs. Bilder nodded, still talking about how bad Arlington-Zack was. There was someone else in another stall—Jess could hear the sound of peeing—and usually Jess tried to be alone in the bathroom, but she just had to get her knife out right then. As she opened the big blade, she heard flushing, and thought the other girl would wash her hands and go out, but suddenly she heard a little scream and when she looked up, the girl's head was poking over into her stall. She was standing on the toilet seat, spying.

"Stop it!" said Jess, closing her knife so quickly she almost cut herself. She put it back in her pocket. "Don't spy on me!"

"You have a knife!" the girl said. Jess didn't know her name. She was in Aaron's class, the one with a man teacher.

"So what!" said Jess. "It's mine!"

"I'm telling!" the girl said, jumping down and busting out of the bathroom. She didn't even wash her hands. Jess got out of there, too, and was on her way out of the building when Mrs. Bilder caught up with her and grabbed her shoulder and made her go into the nurse's room.

"Give it to me," she said, holding out her hand. The nurse watched them, an interested look on her face. At first Jess shook her head, but Mrs. Bilder just stood there staring at her, and finally Jess took out her knife and put it in the teacher's hand. Both Mrs. Bilder and the nurse gasped. Tears came up in Jess's eyes.

"So *that's* what you had in your pocket!" said Mrs. Bilder, holding up Jess's knife like it was a dead rat. "I knew it was something. Young lady, I have been teaching second grade for over forty years and have never once known a child to bring something this dangerous to school. We'll see what the principal has to say to you, and we'll certainly be calling your parents. Follow me."

And the principal called Mugsy and Mugsy had to leave the library to come to the school, and everyone talked and talked at her and the principal said she was sorry but there were rules about bringing a weapon to school and there was nothing she could do about it, and Mugsy took Jess home and called Ka-chan, and Ka-chan had to leave graduate school and come home and they talked and talked at her and when they were finally finished, Jess went up to her room and threw all her whittling sticks out of the window because the principal had kept her knife and she didn't know if she would ever see it again.

CHAPTER NINE:
THE NEW DEAL

"I just can't believe it!" wailed Mugsy, walking up and down the kitchen floor. "I just can't believe this happened!"

"Honey, stop." Ka-chan was taking this much more calmly than Mugsy. It was way after supper and the twins were asleep. Jess was supposed to be asleep, too, but she was sitting on the stairs, just out of reach of the light coming from the kitchen, spying. She couldn't sleep. She missed her knife, she missed Oni, and she knew Mugsy and Ka-chan would be talking about what had happened today at school.

"It's just so ridiculous!" moaned Mugsy.

"Keep your voice down! She's probably still awake, poor child." Ka-chan looked out the kitchen door and Jess hunkered down as much as she could. "It's no big thing, Melanie."

"They *suspended* her, Yuki!" Mugsy was not keeping her voice down. "They suspended an eight-year old for carrying her own possession in her own pocket!"

"A knife, which she was opening in the bathroom. She scared that other girl."

"A miserable, spying little tattletale!" Mugsy said furiously.

"Come here, *chibi*." Ka-chan opened her arms and Mugsy went and sat on her lap. The kitchen chair creaked but held.

"Am I too heavy?" Mugsy asked into Ka-chan's neck, and Ka-chan said, in her lovey voice, "Not in the least. You feel good." They sat there for a long time and Jess was afraid they were going to start kissing, but finally Mugsy sighed and got up from Ka-chan's lap to sit in her own chair.

"I know she's not supposed to have her knife at school," she said. "Stupid rule, if you ask me—it's not like it's a machete!—but whatever. It's just when I got the call from the principal and she was all, 'I'm sorry, but this is the protocol I have to follow,' I just remembered why we wanted to homeschool in the first place, to stay clear of all those restrictive rules. And now I don't know what to do!"

"We'll do what we always do, Mel," said Ka-chan. "We'll figure this mess out."

After that, they said a lot more, but Jess had started to feel very sleepy, so she went back to bed. In the morning, she didn't have to go to school. She wasn't *allowed* to go to school. She had done something so bad that they didn't want her in school for three whole days! Her moms said the consequence that she was getting from them, for disobeying and breaking her promise not to take her knife to school, was no knife until the new year, even if Mrs. Epsilon did give it back. Instead of going to school, Jess went to work with Mugsy at the library and spent the day reading in the children's room.

On Mugsy's break, they went across the street to buy a snack from the convenience store, and they ate it in the garden next to the library. Jess got peanut butter crackers and Mugsy got a Coke. "Don't tell Ka-chan, and I'll let you have a sip," she said.

The next day, Jess went to grad school with Ka-chan. She had her book and she sat in the back of the class, planning to read while a professor gave a lecture, but the lecture was about a kind of person who lived in the rainforest and it was very interesting. Afterwards, she and Ka-chan were talking all about the interesting lecture, and Ka-chan said maybe Jess would be an anthropologist when she grew up, too. Jess usually thought she was going to be a farmer, but she didn't say anything because Ka-chan seemed so excited. They went to a cafeteria and got a snack. Jess got peanut butter crackers, and Ka-chan got a coffee drink called a latte. "Don't tell Mugsy, and I'll let you have a sip," she said. Neither the Coke nor the latte were very good, but it was funny that the moms were keeping food secrets from each other.

The third day, Jess went to the library with Mugsy again. The fourth day was Saturday, and as soon as everybody was up and had had pancakes, the E-Ps had a family meeting. They took care of regular business first, like what people wanted for supper the coming week, if anyone had any complaints or compliments or suggestions for the management, and what the plan was for the weekend, which was: hang out at home today, do some chores, watch a movie and have pizza tonight, go to church on Sunday morning and then go for a short hike Sunday afternoon. Then the twins were excused to go play Lego in the rumpus room, and Mugsy told Jess that they were having an extra special family meeting, just the moms and her. Jess felt worried and excited in her stomach.

"So Jess, do you have anything you want to say?"

"I don't want to go back to that school!" Jess said, and her nose got tickly and her eyes began to have some tears.

"Oh, baby," said Mugsy. "Let's go sit on the

couch." They did, the three of them snuggling up together, Jess in the middle.

"So Mugsy and I have been talking and thinking hard about what happened," said Kachan. "And we have a question for you. If you knew you could homeschool again in a couple of months, would you be willing to go back to school until then?"

"What do you mean?" asked Jess. She loved hearing the magic word "homeschool" but didn't ever, ever want to go back to Mrs. Bilder's class.

"We're doing some research and we've found some homeschoolers who live in the area," said Kachan. "But we're not quite set up enough yet to be able to pull you out of school. We don't have things all worked out, but we're getting closer. We think there's a way you could homeschool with some other kids, but we don't want to go full-speed-ahead until we're sure of what's out there. The other thing that might happen is that Maureen might start homeschooling Zack. Then the two of you could do stuff together. How does that sound?"

"Why is *he* going to homeschool?" asked Jess.

"Well, I don't know if you noticed, but Maureen says he really has trouble in school. With bullying, I guess. But this isn't about him, Jess; it's about you. What do you think? Could you go back and be brave and stick it out until we get something set up for you? Could we have a deal like that?"

"A New Deal?" asked Jess. Her stomach was still excited and her heart was excited now, too.

Mugsy and Ka-chan laughed. "Right on, girl!" said Ka-chan. "A New Deal!"

"How long will it take you to figure this out?" asked Jess. She had a better idea.

"I don't know. A month?" Mugsy looked at Ka-chan, who nodded and said, "That sounds about right."

"Instead of school, could I go live with Litka until you're ready?" The words shot out of Jess's mouth and bounced around the room. From the expressions on her moms' faces, it was clear they hadn't even considered that particular scenario.

"Sweetheart, we would miss you too much!" blurted out Mugsy, but Ka-chan looked thoughtful.

"That's an interesting idea," she said. "Wouldn't you be lonely for us? We would be lonely for you!"

Jess shrugged. It wasn't a good choice: Vermont or her family. "Yes, but I could come back to Arlington right away as soon as you knew about the homeschooling."

An Episode was brewing in the rumpus room, and the moms could no longer ignore it.

"To be continued," said Mugsy, jumping up and yelling, "Boys! Cut it out! Time for chores!"

Ka-chan stayed sitting with Jess for a minute. "Have you been talking with Litka about this?" she asked, hugging her. Jess shook her head. "No, it just seems like a good idea."

"It's not a bad idea at all. It's pretty creative, given everything that's going on. But we'll have to do some really careful planning."

The planning might have been careful, but it didn't take very long. In just a few days, Jess was all set up to go back to Morrisville and stay with Litka and her mom for a couple of weeks. Then she would come back and start homeschooling with Arlington-Zack. Maureen told Mugsy and Ka-chan that she was inspired by them to give her son a better childhood experience than getting bullied and punished all the time. Jess hoped that they would do more than just play on the PS2, but anything was better than the classroom of Mrs. Bilder.

"Do you think I can have some playdates with Sarah, though?" she asked Mugsy. Sarah had called her twice since she'd been out of school.

"Of course," said Mugsy. "And any of the other friends you made at Brackett. And we'll still be seeing the fictive kin a lot, too."

The E-P family was going to drive up to Morrisville to drop Jess off on a three-day weekend called Columbus Day. Mugsy and Ka-chan hated

Columbus Day because they said nobody had discovered America and there had already been people living here and Columbus wasn't a nice man at all. Her moms often had a very different version of history than other people.

"It will be good to visit back home a little," said Mugsy.

"And see how Marc and Renee are getting along in Holy Smoke," said Ka-chan.

"Uncle Marc better not have done any painting!" said Jess. She liked the story about the time Uncle Marc had painted his room dark purple when he was a teenager. Jess actually thought it sounded pretty, but no one would let her change the color of her room, not at Holy Smoke and not in Arlington.

It made her feel really weird to remember that she was going back to Morrisville but not to live in Holy Smoke. She kept having to remind herself about that. She knew Litka's house like the back of her hand and had spent whole weekends there before, but going to live there was another thing altogether. Better than going to school, though. Sometimes she would think of Mrs. Bilder by accident and get a shiver.

The drive to Vermont was like all of their road trips, with several pit stops and one explosion from Ka-chan, who was driving, when the twins wouldn't stop fighting. She pulled over into a rest stop and made everyone get out of the car and take laps around the parking lot until steam had been blown off. Finally, finally, they got there. Leaves were starting to turn colors and it was much cooler than in Arlington. They turned down the driveway to Holy Smoke and there were Uncle Marc and Aunt Renee waiting for them. Uncle Marc had on his jester hat with all the tassels and bells, and he was jumping up and down and waving. They were home.

As soon as she could get someone to drive her, Jess went straight to Far Out Orchard and Farm. Lulu was waiting for her in the lower field with the tractor.

"He's working the upper pasture, with the teenage lambs," she said. "Hop on." She looked at Jess carefully. "You're taller," she said. "Want to drive?" All the kids had learned to drive the tractor last year, and of course Jess wanted to drive. Lulu pulled her onto her lap and handed over the controls. They putt-putted along. Lulu didn't say a lot—she never did—but she kept her hands draped loosely around Jess's waist in a friendly way.

Jess stopped the tractor at the fence and they jumped off.

"See him?" asked Lulu.

Jess had to look carefully, but then there he was, lying down keeping a close eye on the sheep, blending in with the grasses and weeds. His head was on his paws and his ears were up.

"Oni!" she whispered, so quietly he never could have heard her, but his ears swiveled and he lifted his head.

Lulu put her fingers in the corners of her mouth and made the short, short, long whistle that told Oni he could stop his job and come over. He was up and flying across the field before the shrill noise had stopped, and then he jumped up against Jess's chest. She let him knock her over, laughing, falling and rolling with him, feeling his tongue on her eyelids and up her nose and in her ears and across her lips, smelling his Oni breath and kissing him back all over. He was barking and she was crying, and her secret fear dissolved in the autumn air and floated away on the breeze.

"You remember me!" she told him in his ear, grabbing him and wrestling him to the ground, scrubbing his belly with her fist. "You remember me, Oni!"

Of course he did.

THE END

THANKS FOR READING!

Oni kisses and bear hugs from Mugsy for anyone who finds typos or editorial mishaps and send us the info at lazcfemme@gmail.com!

ACKNOWLEDGEMENTS

Thank you to my sons Riley and Liam, who actually grew up in Arlington playing stickball, going to Brackett and spending time at Robbins Farm Park, and who were fact checkers and suggestion givers throughout the writing of this book. Riley wrote the rules!

Thank you to my spouse, Duck, who is a loon from Vermont despite having been born in Texas, and who wholeheartedly supports my writing and believes in me. She fact checked the Vermont parts. I love you!

Thank you to Moe DePinto at metaldetector.com who gave me a good visual of a metal detector and who suggested the pine tree shilling would be a great find. He's the expert, and any fantasy is purely my own doing!

Thank you to my Laz-E-Femme Team: Michael Mahin for his artful design and help with the technology. You are fabulous, Michael, and I couldn't have done it without you! Skye Murie for conjuring up Jess and her family —especially Oni! -- with such love and care. Your illustrations add such depth and beauty to the book! Mel Goldsipe your editorial acumen is a blessing. My dear friend and sister writer, Milva DiDomizio, your eagle eye detected typos and you kept me honest about homeschooling. *Thanks to Oakes Plimpton for inspiring The Old Guy!*

Thank you to AnitaCristina Calcatera's 4th grade class at Brackett who invited me to read them the chapter "Frownie Face" and who had many excellent comments and ideas. Oliver Phillips, Reese Lynch, Shane McCarron, Ben Lau, Jake Riley, Liam Childs, Kevin Yuan, Claudia Wolfe, Elise Kempf, Grace Von Zahcm, Julia McNeill, Maya Pollack, Lisa Turicohia, Lucy Spellmeyer, Nick Diplacido, Austin Cassia, Elyse Spink, Lindsey Bledsoe, Greta Mastro, Kathleen Simmons, and Cate Butler: you're in the book, people!

Ms. Calcatera's 2016-2017 class also gets a great big thank you. They kindly welcomed me to read them the whole book. *and* They are *also* wonderful writers and illustrators in their own right, *too* and had many excellent comments and ideas. Thanks to: Andrew *and we are thrilled to feature their art on the Laz-E-Femme website.*

125

Beck, Max Connor, Charles Curran, Samuel Davis, Leo Fenollosa, Sophia Francis, Peter Harrison, Mackenzie Keenan, Ian Lewis, Holly Moylan, Mireia Nokes, Benjamin Pierce, Nicholas Rudolph, Nolan Russell, Fiona Saunderson, Edallen Severe, Lila Toulmin, Elyse Wagner, Calvin Wood, Gavin Yunes and Annika Ziegler.

Deep gratitude to my heroes, Lee Lynch and John Preston, whose love of our people pushed them to write our stories and write some more.

And finally, thank you to Devon Haessler, who asked a long time ago for a chapter book about a family like hers.

BIBLIOGRAPHY

Irish Tales and Sagas, edited by Ulick O'Conner

Wolves of Willoughby Chase and *Night Birds on Nantucket* by Joan Aiken, books 1 and 3 of *The Wolves Chronicles*

Mrs. Piggle Wiggle series by Betty MacDonald

Mrs. Pepperpot series by Alf Proysen

Native American Animal Stories told by Joseph Bruchach

The Ramona Quimby & Henry Higgins books by Beverly Cleary

Stickball rules

TEAMS usually played on concrete such as parking lot
or basketball court outside.
• Good places are schools especially on weekends
when parking lot is empty.
• Need a couple of tennis balls and a bat

rules

• Games are seven innings or any other agreed
upon amount.
•

• pitcher does lob pitches
- No called strikes or balls.
• game is played with the field it cleanly
rule which is that if a batter hits a ground
ball and the fielder fields it without dropping
it the batter is out.
~~   ~~

• If ball is hit high enough to be a pop fly
the field it cleanly rule does not apply.
The fly ball must be caught in the air.
• No catchers and no stealing or leaving
• pegging is allowed to get the runner out.
• If the fielder misses the peg the runner is
allowed one base on an overthrow if the ball goes
out of play.
• Innings are played with two outs instead of
three.

Teams
can
consist
of
2 to
9 players
depending
of
field
size

→

bigger?
darker.

128

Round Robbin Stickball

- Game can be played with 3 people.
- Each player is on their own team.
- They take turns batting.
- ~~The batter goes first.~~ There is a batter, fielder, and pitcher.
- After a round which is when the batter gets out twice the batter goes to fielder. The fielder to pitcher and pitcher to batter.
- After a hit there is a ghost runner on the base.
- Ghost runners can only run as many bases as the next hit is. EX. If a ghost runner is on 2nd and a player hits a single there is then a runner on 3rd and 1st. If a player hits a double then the ghost runner advances 2 bases which makes it score.
- ✗ All other rules follow regular stickball rules.

✗ Cool thing about stickball is that you can create your own field anywhere!

Night At the Museum

Choose 1 person to be guard. Place the rest in a position. The guard plays role up looking out nothing moves. If the guard sees someone move they are out. If the guard has not see nothing, they stays in.

Andrew   Feb 2, 2017